The
Happy
Hotline

The Happy Hotline

To Be, Or To Convince Others Not To Be

Joe Kuttler

For the boys of the 8, the Slope,
BT and South Forest,
who helped me get through
tough times.

Foreword: Please Don't Kill Yourself

This book will get dark. It is an exercise in exploring nihilism, the idea that life is meaningless. Many characters will face the worst the world has to offer, and many of them will suffer. And many will succumb to their suffering.

I have a deep fear that someone, even one person, might read my story and succumb to the temptations of nihilism and self-destruction that I outline in this book. For this reason, I have written this foreword. There is a chance that people might misinterpret my story, or that I have written it in an unmasterly way wherein the conclusion I have drawn is ambiguous to the reader, and for my own lack of writing skill the reader might be encouraged to succumb to their demons.

But as I look out into the world and see the abject hopelessness on so many people's faces, my greatest fear is that I will not have the courage to print this book. While I recognize the potential danger in publishing a work that explores what happens when a man loses all meaning in life, I believe that by meeting this man face to face we can better understand him and find meaning in our own lives. By doing so, I hope to bring these issues of mental health and suicide to the forefront. I hope that shining a spotlight on these issues will lead to greater empathy in the reader and a greater understanding for the struggles that many people experience. I also hope that readers who have faced the challenges of mental health will gain something from reading about my journey confronting similar challenges.

I wrote this book to test myself and my beliefs. My greatest, most long-held belief is that life is worth living. The flipside to this belief is that I believe that the nihilistic approach is wrong. These beliefs were intrinsic to my upbringing and are intrinsic to both my character and my soul. This novel is a challenge to the idea that life is inherently meaningful, and an embrace of the possibility that the nihilistic approach might indeed withhold great truth.

I approached this challenge at a particularly opportune time, while reeling from a painful breakup. I embraced the possibility that life was not worth living. I told myself that those whom I loved would always leave me, that I would never find love again, that I'd die sad and alone, and that I would never accomplish anything that I aspired to accomplish. With these thoughts in mind, I wrote this novel.

Over the course of this novel I draw out different versions of myself: the hopeless romantic, the idealist, the environmentalist, the farmer, the builder, the veteran, the son, the sinner, the one who hopes to be absolved of his sins. And, over the course of the novel, I kill off all these versions of myself until there is only one me left: the truest, deepest me. This is the version of myself for whom I must live. Or not.

And now, as I write this foreword, I stand on the other side, having completed the novel. What have I gained? If anything, I have greater empathy for people who have lost, or have never found, their meaning in life, and who are tempted to succumb to the great pain inherent in living a life one finds meaningless. Life is indeed a struggle. Yet in this struggle we might also find meaning.

Viktor Frankl, a psychiatrist, author and concentration camp survivor, argued in his book *Man's Search for Meaning,* that people can endure suffering, so long as they find meaning in their suffering. This emphasis on finding meaning in not only the successes, but also the difficulties of one's life, held great significance to Frankl. He contended, in contrast to Friedrich Nietzsche's will to power and Sigmond Freud's will to pleasure, that man's deepest need for fulfillment was the will to meaning. Frankl found that his fellow concentration camp inmates who could maintain hope vastly improved their chances of survival. They maintained their hope through finding meaning in their perseverance against the Nazis. Those who gave up their hope had no chance to overcome the brutality they faced.

We live during quite different times than Frankl did. However, the human condition remains the same, both in times of grotesque war and in times of peace. Therefore, we too, when we feel our suffering is meaningless, are ill-equipped to persevere. Sometimes, we even consider suicide.

To confront why we must discuss suicide, I pose this question: Why are suicide rates currently high? If life is and always has been a struggle, why does it seem like we're failing in our struggles more than our ancestors did in theirs? I attribute our submitting rather than overcoming our struggles to a lack of community. For millennia, humans have found meaning through their connection with other people and the world around them. Community, while sometimes castigating individuals and leading them to isolation, more frequently brings people together. In this togetherness, man has frequently found meaning.

I also attribute our growing discontent to how far from nature many of us live. We evolved as hunters and gatherers, then as farmers. Only recently have we lived in a true white-collar economy, where most of our labor is done indoors. Because we are so disconnected from nature, we have increasingly destroyed both it and ourselves.

However, it's not too late to live more in

accordance with nature and with our fellow humans. This means spending more free time outdoors, with other people; going for hikes with friends and stopping to wonder at and commune with the plants, animals and people we meet along the way. We can go to farmers markets to meet the people who grow our food, asking them about their crops and learning what kinds of foods, drinks and medicines are derived from them that can enhance both our diets and our lives. We can shop small and forge relationships with local crafts people and small business owners. We might spend more money, but we'll get a better product that will last longer. We'll feel good about supporting a friend's business and about knowing where the products we use in everyday life are made, and who made them. We can join running clubs, book clubs and any other club of interest, or simply talk to random people on the street. We can ask them about their lives and tell them about ours.

These recommendations aren't easy. They take social risk and investment. They can be daunting. But they almost always reap great rewards and often return strong dividends. We find meaning in our relationships and in creating something for ourselves and for others. These strong relationships are worth striving for. No one can go through the world alone. It is too hard of a world to do so.

Now, is a lack of community and meaningful

human connection the only reason people commit suicide? No. But almost any hardship can be overcome with the help of others. And many of our problems today do stem from feeling like we don't matter, which frequently occurs when we don't have those important human connections. That's why I so strongly encourage them.

So, when we venture forth into the world, let's make sure that we do so with a community. Let's not wander into the wilderness alone, but rather venture into nature with others. Eventually, we might forget how much we currently struggle with this great question of whether life is worth living. It might always be a question worth asking, but perhaps one day we'll have found enough meaning in life, and rebuilt our communities so strongly, that we'll forget it was so large an issue in the first place. And people like me won't have to write such dark, distressing books.

Mental Health Resources

Luckily for all of us, real suicide hotline operators are nothing like the character detailed in this book. They are kind, patient, empathetic, and save lives every single day. Below are mental health resources. Please, do not hesitate to seek help.

To bolster the efforts of these organizations, $1 will be donated for every book sold.

National Suicide Prevention Lifeline:
1-800-273-8255
National Alliance on Mental Illness:
1-800-950-6264 or info@nami.org
Mental Health America
The Mental Health Coalition
Movember (Men's Health)
The Trevor Project (For LGBTQ youth, friends, and family)
Veterans Crisis Line (For veterans, service members, National Guard and Reserve, friends, and family)

The
Happy
Hotline

"Suicide – however much may already have been said or done about it – is an event of human nature that demands everyone's sympathy, and it should be dealt with anew in every era."

– Johann Wolfgang von Goethe

CHAPTER ONE

"I'm glad you decided to throw out the noose, Joseph. There's a nice full moon out tonight. Why don't you put on your coat and go for a nice stroll? Feel the frigid air shock your lungs. Embrace the cold until your body begs you to return indoors. Take a piping hot shower and collapse into bed. Tune out that recurring dream where you're standing naked in front of your old boss's desk.

"Wake up refreshed. Remember to smile at the rising sun. Put on a button-down and your favorite pair of slacks. Make yourself a nice hash or some bacon and eggs. Keep sending out those emails to prospective employers. You're going to be fine. I promise. Don't give up. I'm always here if you ever need to talk; you have my personal number. Be well... Okay, no problem, have a good night."

I placed the phone gently back onto the desk. It made a soft click. Deep breath in. Hold it. Let it out. In again. And out. And in again. And out again.

Check off the box on the Hotline Helpers checklist. Check all the remaining boxes. Smile. Another soul has successfully been saved.

Too many needed saving. I leaned back in my chair and waited for the next one to call.

It got tiring pulling them all back from the brink. I had successfully set Joseph out to stagger down those icy Minneapolis streets, frozen hands thrust into his body reaching for a nearly extinguished inner fire. And it felt good to save him, and all the others.

But there were heaps more. So many more. They never stopped calling, demanding you listen to them and give them your attention, even though their stories were all just variants of each other.

To be honest, I'd gotten numb to their pain. Sometimes, I even felt bored.

To be fair to Joseph and the rest of them, we were in the middle of a long and brutal winter. The Mississippi was entombed in the winter's clasp. The river couldn't recall a time when it wasn't frozen, and Joseph could no longer see the fish swimming below the crusted surface. Neither he nor the river remembered warm spring days full of bare-chested joggers and soaring eagles. Even I could barely remember those days, and they were all I thought about.

The sun was both months behind us and months away. It was yet the dead of winter. The endless season of interminable nights. It was so dark I could barely spot the frozen river through the window. It felt like suicide numbers were only so low because so many people froze to death before they could even think about killing themselves.

I shivered and closed the window. Luckily, everything was warm and bright inside the House of the Hotline. The yellow walls were full of murals. Rainbows and dandelions floated above green fields surrounded by cedar and oak trees. Deer families skipped and hopped through towers of corn.

Big candy cane lollipops waited for Christmas at the entrance to the meeting room, where interminable life-affirmation mantras were chanted once a week as everyone sat in a circle holding hands, heads turning back and forth to neighbors, mouths espousing compulsory love.

You are loved. You are loved. No, really, YOU are loved. Who, me? Aw, shucks. Really, though, **you** are loved. Thank you so much for saying that. No, thank **you**.

Then everyone would lay down on the floor, feet splayed to either side, so everyone's ankles were draped over everyone else's. Close your eyes and feel the festering smell of love in the air.

The phone rang again. Deep breath in. Hold. Deep breath out. Life is for living. Big, fat smile.

"Hello there, friend. How are you feeling today?"

"Um… not too well, I guess."

I skimmed the encouraged script. I'd been doing my best to stay within the required confines of the script, while still making the experience as entertaining for myself as I could. Keeping myself entertained was the only thing keeping me from succumbing to the brutal malaise I got listening to so many people's dreadful stories.

"Where would you say you are on your Sad to Happy Meter if sad is a penguin stuck in a boiling desert and happy is if Gary Anderson hit the kick against the Falcons, so we would've made the Super Bowl?"

"Who's Gary Anderson?"

"You mean you don't know the former Vikings kicker who's the biggest pariah in the state? Sorry, you are calling from the Twin Cities, right?"

"Yeah. I'm over in St. Louis Park."

"Okay, well, let's start over. What's your name?"

"Yossi."

"Hi Yossi, my name is Jay. How long have you been feeling down, Yossi?"

"I guess just a few days… But I guess really a couple months. I don't know. Chava left me."

"And who is Chava?"

"She was my fiancé."

"Okay, so Chava left you, maybe a couple of months ago, but you've been feeling really down for the last couple of days, correct? What happened a couple days ago?"

"Um… I guess we were just going to meet up and talk. I knew what she was going to say but I knew what I hoped she was going to say and that was the truth that I was counting on if that makes any sense. And I had thousands of conversations with her in my head over the last few weeks, or I guess the last couple of months, since we sat together crying when she broke up with me. I cried real tears, the first time I cried since middle school, before my Bar Mitzvah, before the army, before everything, before I was even a real person. She told me she just needed a short break. It was hard but I thought we had a great base that we'd built together and could make it through anything. And we'd reunite in a few weeks when she was ready."

I buckled into my seat. This guy was already on a roll and I could tell he'd keep me on the phone a while. He barely remembered to breathe as he gushed out his story. Meanwhile, I put chap stick on my cracked lips.

"I used to live with her family. My mom and I had a falling out a couple years back just after my dad died and around the time Chava and I started dating and her parents gave me my own room to stay in. I got really close with her parents and her sisters and their husbands. They made me feel like I was in their family. Their dog Gus loved me and ran up to me whenever I came back from work. I loved her and she said she loved me. We used to go on long walks together and we never ran out of things to say to each other and she was so fun to be with and I made her laugh all the time and got to see her little teeth emerging from behind those beautiful lips I used to kiss all the time."

I put myself on mute. My foot's tapping had started to echo in the receptacle. Yossi was one of those people who'd tell you their whole life story the second you feigned interest. Of course, I wasn't feigning interest and it was indeed my job to listen, but get to the point, man. We get it; you're depressed. So's everyone else. Wrap it up so I can remind you how to be happy and help save the next guy. So many others needed my help.

"In the beginning of our relationship she was in such a dark place. It was like she had these storm clouds sitting over her waiting to let loose on her all the time but I couldn't see them and she couldn't either except for when they were all she could see and then she was trapped and I couldn't get through to her. It was hard but I helped her crawl out of that dark pit and we danced and laughed and loved each other so much. When she moved to Tucson for medical school last fall I helped her get settled there with her roommate and then I flew back home to set off on my travels. I went off to Australia and New Zealand and we talked every day even when the time difference was something insane like 15 or even 18 hours and every beautiful place I went I always wished she was there to see the kangaroos and koalas and waterfalls with me and lead me holding my hand jumping into lakes and oceans together but it was okay because I could still share those places with her even over the phone."

He kept going on and on as the wind howled against the windows.

It was indeed a brutal winter. Not only for Joseph and Yossi but for the whole town. The Vikings had lost again, to the fucking Packers. The Mississippi froze, which hardly ever happened. Commuters would drive to work in the dark and return home in the dark. The Northern Lights, which sometimes appeared to make

the long nights at least a little brighter, were nowhere
to be seen. There was a blight of pine trees up north.
Even Big Bob of Bob's Sailboats waited too long to
pull his boats out of the lake and all their sides cracked
from the early layer of ice. It was as if the whole town
had collectively stubbed its toe against the dresser.

"Then I came back home from my travels and
decided I couldn't live without her anymore, so I got
my father's heirloom emerald ring that was his beloved
grandmother's and I asked her dad for her hand in
marriage and we had a serious talk and he advised me
to go back to school and finish my degree and he told
me how he never knew anyone who was successful
without a degree and I said sure thing, I'll seriously
consider it, even though you should really think about
hanging out with some people other than Jewish
doctors and lawyers and accountants but sure, I gotta
provide for her even though she'll be a doctor and be
making good money for herself but we'll figure it out,
money's not a thing, not when it comes to love."

Yossi kept droning on. All these suicidal people
had the same manic energy. I wished I was allowed to
interrupt him to help guide him to his inner peace
already. But it was against Hotline policy.

You see, there are two main types of callers: one
is a chronic caller, someone who battles depression and
anxiety and needs to be cajoled to stay alive nearly
every day. These ones really just need to be heard, since
they have no one else who'll listen to them.

The other type of caller has been plunged so deep

into the pits of despair that he or she considers death a more favorable option to life. This was Yossi. Other hotlines knew to keep these kinds of calls short because once they got rambling, they might convince themselves that they *were* better off ending it all. So, other hotlines would intercept them early in the call to guide them to a safer solution to their issues.

But we at the Happy Hotline were forced to give callers as much time to speak as they wanted. We had to make every caller feel like she had her own personal angel looking out for her, even if it meant leaving dozens of others waiting on hold.

Somehow, it seemed like we did just as well as other hotlines in our success rates. But the pressure on the Hotline Helpers was immense. We had to do some serious heavy lifting to reel these people in after they'd gotten themselves so riled up.

"So, I flew down to her and proposed and God smiled on us and looked down and saw we were happy together and joined at the rib and would be together forever in our perfect garden and I told her she was the love of my life and she was so happy to hear it and kissed me so intensely and I felt her love emanating from every pore of her body flowing up and out through her lips into me. I flew back here because I was still going to work at the farm nearby for a few months until the wedding, when I'd move down there and find a job and we'd move in together. A few months before the wedding I went down to the desert to visit her and I could feel her start to push me away and she said that I never gave her space and that I'd invaded her home and I was doing it again even though she'd always loved having me around and loved how close I was with her family so it made no sense to me. Then she was lamenting that we never had a real flirtatious or build-up period to our relationship but just dove right in and started living together and planning out our lives, like talking about the kind of cabin we would build together by a lake in a pine forest up north and how we'd farm and grow medicinal herbs and build a nice holistic medicine practice for her there in the woods and she'd help people and we'd build a nice community together. But none of that's going to happen now. She said she'd lost romantic interest in me, even with the wedding so near. I was ready for that whole new phase of life and new stage in our relationship and we'd already grown so much together and we could grow so much more and raise kids and grandkids together but she gave up on us."

I wish these people would just go grab a beer at the bar, like they used to. What did they think all the bars were for? It's the Midwest. There were more bars here than anywhere else in the country. There were nothing else to do during those endless, cold, dark nights. It's really not that complicated. Just go drink with your friends and talk about your problems with them.

These people don't get that life is supposed to be hard sometimes. They want to give up the first chance they can. Bars used to be cheaper than going to the therapist, but then Mr. Joey Joy had to show up and create the not-for-pay, just for smiles Hotline, giving free help over the phone whenever anyone felt even a little bit down.

Sure, we charged for our other services, but that didn't help me any when I was stuck on the phone with the countless broken-hearted, beaten-down people of the north who could keep calling as often as they wanted to for free.

"So, we cried together on that last morning, I guess like seven weeks ago now and I had to fly back here and move out of her family's house and move back in with my mom because I didn't have anywhere else to stay and things have been really tense and horrible with her. A couple of days ago I met up with Chava because she was back in town and this whole time I was hoping it was just a break and she'd realize soon enough we were soulmates and come back to me but she told me she had to trust her gut and it was telling her that I wasn't the one for her."

He took a deep breath, then continued. My mind had gone completely blank by this point.

"And that's it. My heart broke into a billion pieces. I'd been hoping she'd figure things out and remember how perfect we were together. But she flung the ring back at me like she was playing fetch with a dog that was completely dependent on her but then I think she felt guilty so she held my hand but then she pulled her hand back and put it back in her lap and there was this unbridgeable chasm between us and I knew that even if I could somehow get her to come back to me, what would be the point? I'd be with someone who'd told me I wasn't the one, so there'd be no more trust or hope anymore. It'd be all fizzled out and burned up and incinerated. I don't want to live without her but I also don't want to always hope she'll come back to me and then close myself off to every other woman on the planet. It all just sucks. And now I'm stuck living back with my mom knowing that I can't see her family ever again since it would be so awkward and horrible and she would hate me for it. I guess I just can't see how I can keep going on. I haven't even been able to force myself to eat for the last two days yet I feel no hunger. I feel like I've lost everything and everyone who mattered to me and cared for me. All that's left is me, but me doesn't matter anymore because there's not one person in the world who values me."

Finally, just when I thought he'd never shut up, he shut up. My eyes had glossed over staring at the wall, so I shook my head to refocus and looked back over the list of necessary information to attain.

"Okay, now Yossi, I have to ask you two questions. One, how long ago did you first consider suicide? Two, do you have a date planned? Oh, and three, I'm going to need you to give me your rating on the Sad-Happy Meter."

"I don't know, zero? Negative fifty? Whatever. I haven't really considered suicide, I guess, it's too hard-wired into my soul that I'm not supposed to do it. But I don't know what to do with my life. I can't eat. I can't sleep. I can only think of Chava and stare at her image plastered on my naked walls in the middle of the night even though I know she's forgotten about me already. I guess if I'm being completely honest I do want it all to end. But I don't really know how I'd do it or if I'd have the guts."

"Oh, so you haven't seriously considered suicide yet?"

"You sound disappointed."

"Oh, no, I'm sorry about that. Just been a long day is all." Now that he'd poured out his soul, I had to conjure something good to help save him. An idea came to me. "I think I might be able to help you out, Yossi. Let me ask you something. Would you consider yourself a religious man?"

"Yes."

I thought my idea might help Yossi, though it bordered the edge of what was allowed for a Hotline Helper to do with a caller. I closed the door to my Happiness Receptacle.

"It's possible I shouldn't do this, but it sounds like you really need my help, and I won't give up on you, Yossi. I think we should do a role-playing game. It'll help you, I'm sure of it. I've heard of therapists using these kinds of games to help others who have struggled just as much as you're struggling now. Okay, let's begin. Are you ready, Yossi?"

"I guess."

"Okay, Yossi. I'm going to tell you something that might sound crazy. You called this number and I told you that you were talking to someone named Jay. That was a lie. You're actually talking to the Creator. It's me, God. I'm so glad that you've brought your troubles to me, Yossi. Let's talk this out. You have a bright future ahead of you. I can see it. And you've been such a devout and righteous man. It pains me to see you hurting so gravely. So, let's help you get back to your path. How does that sound, Yossi?"

"Um … what?"

"Yossi, close your eyes. Take a deep breath. I want you to do something for me, Yossi. Remember, Yossi, this is your Creator talking. This is a commandment, not a request. Okay, Yossi, take a deep breath. Now, I command you to smile. Give me a nice, big smile. You might not know this, Yossi, my son, but I hardwired into your body a nice little trick. Whenever you smile, your brain releases a chemical called dopamine. This dopamine floods your body with happy endorphins. Whenever you feel down, I want you to smile. It's not going to fix everything, it definitely won't bring your fiancé back to you, but it'll do enough to stave off those suicidal feelings. As for how you would commit suicide, it is good that you haven't thought about it too specifically yet. That means that we can easily overcome this Yossi. I just talked someone out of jumping off the Stone Arch Bridge and pulverizing his body on the ice, and I'm going to help you out too, Yossi. Remember, this is your Creator. The all-knowing. I can see the future. I can tell you one thing that will reassure you greatly. Your fiancé is not going to come back to you. That's not the reassuring part. This is: In three years' time you will meet your bride. It's not going to be an easy three years; I won't lie to you. You're going to be miserable and you'll be sad, and you'll want to crawl back to your fiancé begging her to take you back, but she won't, and she's not the one for you. But you will find your soulmate. And she will find you. And you'll both be happy. I promise."

"You're wrong, God! She is the one for me."

"No! Stop that, Yossi. Don't doubt your Creator! Pull yourself together, Yossi. Understand that she wasn't the one for you! The one, your soulmate, the one I signed off on when you were in Heaven before you were born, she'll come to you in three years' time. I promise. Have faith in me."

"I don't know."

"Trust me, Yossi, trust me. The world feels like a big, empty void right now. You feel alone. But you're not. You have your mom. You have your friends. And you will have your love, if you're patient enough for her. You have to step out of that void and join me, and we'll be together, and we'll go and find your partner together. I promise. And you'll be with her together forever."

"Step out of the void. Join you. Together forever. Okay. I'll do that. Thanks."

"No problem, my pleasure. Now, I want you to do something for me. There's a full moon out tonight. Why don't you put on your coat and go for a stroll? Feel the frigid air shock your lungs. Come back home, take a hot shower and get a good night's rest. Remember to smile at the rising sun. Eat a good breakfast tomorrow, maybe make yourself a nice hash or some bacon and eggs. Not bacon, not bacon, how about a bagel with cream cheese and lox? Sounds good, right? You're going to be okay, I'm sure of it. You'll find her soon enough. Never give up. I'm always here if you ever need to talk; my personal number is 881-7773. Be well, son." Click.

Well, that went well. Maybe I shouldn't have mentioned the Stone Arch Bridge. Wouldn't want him getting any ideas. Oh, well. He'll probably call us another five times before he seriously considers doing anything, and by that time he'll have gotten over the roughest part. Let's call it a perfect eight-for-eight tonight.

The shift was just ending. Great timing.

I packed up my things and stood up. My head spun with dizziness. I'd been sitting listening to people's heartaches for so long, it was starting to affect me physically.

I exited my Happiness Receptacle and poked my head into my coworker Hannah's Receptacle.

"All right Hannah, I'm heading out."

"Have a good night Jay. You're always loved."

"No, Hannah, **you're** always loved."

From the artificial glow of the Happy Hotline back onto the dark, blank street. Walking through the parking lot past snow-buried cars, I watched waves of breath steam out of me, which hurried me around the corner to my house.

Back on the couch with a beer in hand, I flicked on the basketball game to witness the Timberwolves' asses handed to them once more.

I turned off the television. The game was already over, even though the second half had only just begun. I finished the beer and shot it into the garbage bin.

The heater was on, but damn, it was still so fucking cold. I pulled off my layers of clothes and crawled into bed, pulling the covers over me. I shivered under the blankets. Winter didn't end until May last year and they've been saying the lakes might not thaw until June this year.

Oh, well. It should keep the lines busy at least. Gotta keep that happiness flowing.

Someone's gotta save those depressed bastards. Those ones who stand alone at the edge of ponds, staring at couples skating hand-in-hand under the moonlight.

And someone's gotta play God, because I sure as shit don't see Him out here.

CHAPTER ONE

The midday sun graced us with its presence. Tepid clouds loomed sparsely on the horizon. Others would join them soon enough, their burgeoning masses conspiring to overcome the sun's gaze. At least, for now, there was no wind.

Jimbo's Bar and Grill stood tall beyond the parking lot, its timber-framed exterior soaking up the sun, welcoming you to shed your coat and scarf and troubles in its warm embrace.

I grabbed a Hamm's from the barkeep and took it out to the patio to enjoy with a smoke, but moms and grandmas running their errands kept casting kind glances my way. It was too early for that, so I headed around back to the loading ramp.

Twin stainless-steel smokers slow-cooked the night's brisket special. I unsheathed a cigarette. A splotchy bearded, apron-clad cook strode over, pumping his arms, accepting a smoke. He cradled a beer in his left hand, clutching the cig in his right.

"Say, are you the guy who cooks up those mean steaks I've been eating here?" I asked.

"Yessir, that's me. Aaron."

"Jay. Nice to meet you. You know, the smell of the meat smoking over there's got me hankering for a nice steak. Would you throw one of those on the grill for me?" He nodded and motioned that he would after he finished his cigarette. "Say, what's that beer you got there?"

"Hite. It's my dad's beer."

He was desperate to tell his story, but hesitated for an instant. He took another drag from his cigarette, looking at me, questioning whether I'd give him the time of day. I looked back at him. The pleasant aroma of the brisket ingratiated him to me, so I nodded at him and buckled in. He plunged on.

"Dad's from Seoul; that's where they brew it. Me and my sister were born there, too. He loved my sister. Then I was born. He left my mom half a year later, and my mom and sister and me had to move back to Cleveland."

"Have you spent any time with him since then?"

"My mom sent me to Seoul to do just that. I was a little boy. Just ten. He met me and we had lunch, some kimchi and kongbap. Then he dropped me off at my aunt's, my mom's best friend in Korea. I stayed there the next three weeks waiting for him to come pick me up again. But he wouldn't see me. I cried so much waiting for him."

His face was hardened with years of seeking love from a man who didn't care for him, but his boyish eyes sought approval in my own.

"Mi-sook, my aunt, took me to see the sights and

wanted to fly with me to show me Jeju Island. But I wouldn't leave Seoul in case my dad decided to see me. He didn't, so I flew back home, and then, when I turned 15, I started drinking Hites because that's where I come from."

He took another deep swig from the Hite.

"I went to college for a bit. Studied economics. But then I made friends with some cooks at my local bar in Cleveland and started the kitchen life. I moved to New York City with my buddy James. We were an apartment of cooks, five of us. The cooking life's real back east. Cook til 2, 3 A.M. Head over to a buddy's bar and drink til 5 or 6. Get some sleep. Then head back to the bar at 10:30 in the morning to start prepping for the next night. Lots of highs and lows living like that. Me and James would get depressed pretty bad. I struggle with depression …"

He trailed off, suddenly conscious that he'd been pouring out his soul to me, a total stranger. He was but one of the millions of lonely people waiting to spill their guts out the second they could find a pair of ears; their own antennae flared skyward, dials tuned to dispatch, receivers off.

Some would gather at the bar to commiserate, hoping to find someone to listen. A growing number of others were too racked by social anxiety to even venture into the bars, so they'd retreat home and flick on screens blaring voices at them.

Don't dare shut it all off. Then the thundering silence will crash down, trapping your thoughts in a vacant, untamed savannah. Leave the static on to descend easier into sleep.

Even though I spent all my working hours listening to these people, these human transmitting machines, I could tell that Aaron needed to get it all out, to be heard for once, so I nodded to him again to continue.

"We'd discuss whether life was worth living, me and James. If it was, what should we do about it? If it wasn't, what should we do about it? It's tough because there's a billion different ways to go for the first one, but only one answer for the second."

My professional instincts kicked in. "Have you ever been tempted to find that answer for yourself?"

He looked off into the distance. "Well, I won't lie to you, it's crossed my mind. When Anthony Bourdain did it, it hit me hard. He was my cooking god. I read his book. Took me a while to get over it when he did it. I thought that if he couldn't keep going, and he was at the pinnacle of the cooking profession, what chance did I have?"

His gaze remained focused on some distant, unseen point. It seemed like he was considering whether he'd made the right choice to continue, even when his hero had taken the opposite approach. His shoulders sagged.

"A few weeks ago, my mom left me a message, crying that Mi-sook died in a car accident. My whole family flew back to Seoul for her funeral. But I'd lost my phone like the bum that I am and didn't get the message in time. When I finally got it, they were already back home from Korea."

He took two deep puffs of the cig, then flicked it far down the ramp with his middle finger.

"My first job was at a Wendy's, frying shit. Then I worked at some dives and learned to grill. Now I'm good; really good, actually. But cooking's not a life. I'm 35. Making 14 an hour. No benefits. I can't really make it work like that."

My stomach started rumbling. I was hoping he'd wrap it up and start cooking my steak, but he kept going.

"My car broke down a few weeks back. Had to put a new transmission in it. Then some plastic bullshit corroded on the coolant connection. Had to sink more money into that. That shit adds up, you know? Had to buy the new phone. I don't know if I can keep doing this, but cooking's the only thing I know how to do. It's the only thing I really like doing. Thing is, I keep bouncing from bar to bar, so there's not really any promotions or anything in it."

He tanked the Hite bottle and tossed it into the dumpster.

"They don't mind you drinking while you cook?"

"Only way to cook, bud. Let me go grill you up that steak."

He headed into the kitchen and I walked back into the restaurant.

Wine glasses hung upside down from the liquor cabinets beneath the high oak trusses, full of half-empty bottles of cheap whiskey clustered like bowling pins ready to be decimated. Aaron grabbed a glass of Jack from the bartender and hurried back into the kitchen.

It was a good fucking steak. Nice and bloody. I sent back another glass of Jack to Aaron and headed off to the House of the Hotline.

At the start of the driveway an infuriatingly happy, red-afroed, green-nosed, incandescent clown smiled resolutely against the bitterness of the world. The driveway was dotted with kaleidoscopic, bubble-lettered slogans: CHIN UP, COWBOY. And: FOCUS ON THE GOOD. Or: YOU'RE THE CHAMP. The classic: THE SUN WILL COME OUT TOMORROW. And my personal favorite: LIFE IS FOR LIVING! SMILE! These slogans rang so unbelievably fake it was a wonder anyone made it to the building without severing their femoral artery.

The hotline was housed in a shiny three-story stucco building painted with the blues, whites, and oranges of Miami and the Caribbean. Its beach was a mangled corpse of snow piles ebbing in and out with the winter winds. Vendors hawked hot chocolate and apple cider to the empty-eyed beings thrust into the building's glow of Happiness.

The Happy Hotline wasn't your run of the mill suicide hotline; it was an all-encompassing shelter for those masses devastated by the raging storms of society. People came here for crayon therapy, for guided meditation, for goat yoga, for forgetting their misery and everyone else's happiness, for feeling like they weren't alone in their misery, for getting through another day, not even a day, for getting through another minute.

It made little sense that so many people turned to a suicide hotline to meet their health and wellness needs. I know I wouldn't choose to spend so much time in so morbid a place if they weren't signing my paycheck. My best guess was that people were so starved for any semblance of a community that we served as their last resort.

You might think that because so many people needed our help that everyone around here was depressed. But Minnesota's actually a very happy place. Which was exactly the problem.

Minnesotans are deeply rooted in Scandinavian genetics, culture and emotions. The frozen tundra of northern Europe and the uppermost reaches of our country don't necessarily cause a higher rate of suicide than anywhere else. But the ones who do anguish suffer so much more in their misery. They make Mediterranean slashers of wrists and Andean hangers of necks seem like veritable celebrators of life.

There's something about the combination of everlasting white ground and dark sky. Something about knowing everyone else is happy, about imagining mothers holding toddlers in cozy cabins reading Dr. Seuss, kissing their cheeks at the turn of every page. Teenage girls hug in joyous tears after comically slipping up skating again, while lovers embrace under warm, somehow transparent blankets, letting you imagine their closeness, giving you a vision of interlocked thighs and fingers and tongues. All reminding you of long-forgotten times when you had someone of your own, and someone had you. So, you step outside into the snowy outdoors, but the sun's already set, or it never even bothered to rise, so you step back inside to a million invisible hands refusing to hold you.

The escalators propelled me up into the Hotline complex. Peeking in the direction of the windows, I expected to see the cloudy heavens, but instead faced a projection of a blue summer sky. Somehow, after all this time, I still wasn't used to their damn projections.

Special projector windows lined the walls on the inside of the Hotline from floor to ceiling. Sometimes in the summer the management would let you look outside. The other 300-some days, the windows projected visions of different worlds, worlds of festive beaches and calm oceans, worlds of majestic birds flying over blue lagoons, worlds of aliens in celebration, impossible worlds taunting you with their unreachability.

I stepped into The Fun-Time Room. I still had some "fun"-time to kill until my shift started. Hannah played with her nine-year-old daughter visiting on eternal bring-your-kid-to-work day. The kid ate organic sugarless candy by the handful from an Endless Happiness Jar.

We didn't only combat the peoples' sadness with organic sweets. We offered the public all kinds of joyous possibilities. The eponymous hotline in the Happy Hotline, my own domain, offered our services to the public for free. Everything else came at a cost. However, because we were a non-profit, we didn't make money to make money, we made money to help more people.

A few more of our many offerings included team clap therapy, group cuddle sessions and Buddhist incantation sessions. Alternative services could be provided on a more individualized basis. We could fulfill nearly any of a person's jubilation needs if she had enough money.

"Hey there, Hannah," I said, popping a candy into my mouth. "You're always loved. How's it going?"

Hannah looked up at me from the floor, where she was playing with her daughter. "Hi, Jay. You're always loved! Oh, things are great. We just helped a beautiful old soul get through the loss of his dog. H. was so reluctant to get a new boy, because he would just miss Clifton so darn much, but we had a nice long talk and he decided that he's going to get a new dog to go with his 15 gerbils, 8 mice and 6 cats!"

"The man has 15 gerbils?"

"Oh, yah. He had 30 mice, but then some of the cats were naughty. Now, there's less mice. It took him a while to realize the mice were missing. He ended up having to separate them. He really didn't want to, because it was so nice when the mice and cats got along, but the cats were just too mean and wouldn't learn to play nice."

Hannah, that endless optimist. That eternal, naive believer in the beauty of the world and the wonders of life. Raised in a perfect childhood of jet-ski summers and cozy ice-house winters. Always a fresh batch of chocolate chip cookies on the table to go with a fresh cup of milk. Forever a doting grandparent ready to lavish her with attention and adoration. Her world was always an invisible helping hand.

"Did you hear about that poor man on the bridge yesterday?" she asked.

"What man?"

"They were talking about him on the broadcast system earlier. Sad story, oh yah. He stripped nude on top of the Stone Arch Bridge and leapt off. They said he crushed every bone in his body when he landed on the ice, but he didn't die. He laid there in naked agony until he finally succumbed to hypothermia. Poor soul. He should've called us."

A vision appears to me of Yossi laying naked on the ice. His crushed balls wither up into his body seeking warmth. His shattered limbs spiral in every direction. His cracked mouth shouts blasts of steam into oblivion. Barren eyes. Suffering so great he almost looks at peace. As if he knows the suffering that would've lay ahead of him if he kept living, knowing his destiny having lost his one true love. Putting faith in some absent God to raise him up to Heaven and make things right.

He needed God to show Chava the truth that they were soulmates; they were one soul that God split in Heaven and sent down to Earth to find and love and enrich and fulfill each other and reunite in the lonely plains of the world to become whole once again. To serve and care for each other. Not to give up; never to throw it all away. She'd realize it was the other half of her own soul she gave up on.

Before a god came to save him, Yossi was numb with depression. I could see him lying there splayed out on the ice like a Jewish Jesus on his frozen cross. And he enjoyed this suffering, preferring its intense sting to a lifetime of empty dullness. He basked in his decision until his last breath seeped out of him. A smile rested on his crushed walnut of a face. This smile was a world-changing smile, a smile of peace and surrender. It was a sign, a sign so obvious it was unavoidable. After I received this sign, this north star, I had no choice but to navigate by it.

My epiphany changed everything. It was as if I was born again. Feelings of empathy welled up in me so strongly, I felt I understood every single one of my fellow humans, and I could hear them all calling out to me for help.

Hannah looked at me with her sympathetic eyes. Every word that came out of her mouth seemed as if it emanated from my own soul. Did you hear me, Jay? I was just saying I wish that poor man had given us a call. We could've helped him.

I looked back at Hannah, smiling. I spoke to her

as if discussing an idea with myself, so close did I feel to her, my fellow human. Yup, you're right. I wish he had called. Say, Hannah, do you think that what we're doing is good? Like, is it good we're convincing people to live? Is that small hope of happiness worth sending people back out into the world to return to their wretched miserable lives?

Hannah was taken aback. How can you talk like that? You fill out the Live and Love Questionnaire, just like me, every week. How could it not be good reminding people they want to keep on living? We're not convincing them of it against their will. It's the deepest truth they know. They know it deep down in their hearts and souls, but they've forgotten it because life can get hard and lonesome. It's our job to help them remember.

She could say that, her childhood was perfect. She was endeavoring to form the exact same experience for her own child.

Hannah brightened. Christmas Day's in a week! You know what that means! Peak season's coming up. All those sad people who don't have anyone to buy presents for. I hope you're ready to spread that famous cheer of yours!

The kid butted in. Hannah, let's go play house in the playground. You be the daddy and I'll be the mommy.

Hannah smiled. Okay honey. Just for a little, though. Daddy's got to show the sad people the light they can no longer see.

They left to play the game of life in the indoor playground.

It was time to go punch that clock and hear everyone call in from their lonely, cold lives. So many conversations. They were all dialogues with different manifestations of the self. Each one lives and dies and nourishes the soil for the birth of the next one and the next one and the next one, and some live short miserable lives, and some are doomed to live forever. Some kill and some are euthanized, and they all intermingle and have their place at their appointed times, and they engage in power struggles. Sometimes, the true self emerges and all the other selves are quieted. And sometimes the one true self is diminished, so all the other selves have a field day rampaging wildly about.

I cracked open the window, now revealing three baby gazelles in a mountain skipping and jumping around their mother, to see the incandescent clown glimmering maniacally in the night, forcing people to forget the meaninglessness of their pain. Maybe it was my job to help them remember.

CHAPTER ONE

The trees in the cemetery were naked. A crowd of black-hatted Jews gathered around a frozen pit. The community's patriarchs and matriarchs sat in foldable chairs while the rabbi chanted the prayers. The white ground was packed with snow.

A young woman strode up to the barren tree beside me and leaned her ass against its trunk. We were far enough from the family to give them space to grieve, yet our presence was enough to respect the dead.

I looked again at this woman whose love was so great that the ceasing of it had led her betrothed to suicide. Her face was blank and free of guilt. Her black dress stood out beneath her jacket, dancing in the breeze. She wore sandals on this sunny winter day, the mark of a true girl of the north woods. She glanced in my direction, checking me out.

The bereaved community started filling the hole with dirt. A friend of the deceased, a fellow sufferer of the Earth, stuck his shovel backwards into the pile of dirt, as per tradition, and tossed the first scoop down. Then he turned the shovel right side up and proceeded with the devoted labor of burying his friend.

He should've kept shoveling backwards, lamenting a life given up to hopelessness. A destiny of purgatory awaited poor Yossi. According to Jewish lore, because he'd committed suicide and given up on the life God granted him, ghosts would haunt him six days a week forever. They'd come bearing pitchforks, stabbing into his naked invisible flesh endlessly, taunting him for relinquishing his place on Earth and his eventual ascent up to Heaven.

On the Sabbath, he'd have a brief respite. A time to appreciate the quiet. These singular days validated his decision. He could once a week lie and appreciate his peace. This was his salvation. There would be no comfort any day of the week in his alternate, miserable future.

Chava inhaled from a cigarette. She exhaled the smoke and her breath steamed in the frigid air. She went on inhaling and exhaling the tobacco and the air, and I couldn't differentiate the cigarette smoke from her soul's smoke.

The cigarette dwindled and its ash marred the snow beneath her. She unsheathed another cigarette, handed it to me and leaned her head on my shoulder. Our smoke and steam combined into a dissipating cloud in the air as mourners shoveled dirt over their loved one.

She motioned to me with a sly grin. My boots followed her sunken footsteps in the snow. We snuck into the bathroom, which accepted us into its sanctuary. Mirrorless, the barren room reeked of the sobs, snot and anguish that accompany death when those grieving don't realize the great release it truly is.

Her kisses were tender and longing. Our tongues briefly cavorted. Then she was turned around beneath me, my fingers grasping her naked hips, her hands guiding my member deep inside her.

I crushed her beneath me. She goaded me to take her ever more fully. She needed a powerful force, a refusal to succumb to timidity, a desperation to cling and cleave to life, a cunning life fully lived, taken, ensnared, empowered, seduced, played with, revolted against, a life powerful enough to turn over worlds, forcing them together and separated them and bringing them together again like storm waves crashing upon virgin shores. My arms locked underneath and around her, taking her, pushing her further down and down, grabbing her arms holding them prostrate behind her. Penetrating to her very core.

The eye-level window peered out on snow-covered branches. A naked grove surrounded our refuge. If the trees were clothed with their spring foliage or the reds, oranges and yellows of their autumnal glory, they'd provide no buffer we needed or desired. Her rhapsodic, steady moans grew and grew and I took her stronger and deeper, her back crushed beneath my full force.

She sang like a songbird drunk on overripe berries and her song fluttered out, soaring unrelentingly. Her song was for the dead, the mourning, the community of sufferers, the tombstones, the snow, the naked trees, the descending pile of dirt, the submerged coffin, and the body and bones of the man lying entombed inside it. If you peeked into the window, you'd have seen two hearts beating wildly, four eyes filled with ecstasy, eight limbs entwined in passion, two mouths huffing and puffing, one of them singing, one soul giving itself entirely to an eager receiver from behind.

After her serenade ended and we were again fully clothed, she pulled an apple from her coat pocket and bit from it ravenously. She handed it to me. It was cold, though it had nestled against her warm body just as I had. We shared the fruit, replenishing our voracious bodies.

We returned to the graveside as the last shovelfuls of dirt toppled to the earth. The crowd began dispersing. Cars relented to each other on the narrow cemetery paths.

She handed me a cigarette, told me to wait, and headed over to share obligatory condolences with her could've-been mother-in-law, leaving me leaning once more against a pine. She returned shortly and took my hand, leading me out of the cemetery gates and back into the world.

rises. And winter returns right when summer settles in.

Christmas Eve came too quickly again. The people called in, wanting someone to listen and to care. The Hotline pays empathizers like me $47,287 a year to wind the clocks back and thaw millions of people's estuaries. To convince them that the waters never stopped running, they always have flowed, always would flow.

I lifted the phone to my ear. Hello, sir. How may I help you this bright day? Our windows here at the Hotline project a brighter world. Why don't you come in so I can show you this world? We created it just for you. Oh, you're a fair distance away? Drive down, drive down. No gas money, you say? Well, you've got a credit card, don't you? Overextend that credit if you need to. Get that glimpse of a shiny memory you didn't know you had.

Yes, Aaron? Oh, Aaron. What's this about losing your job? Jim burned down Jimbo's to collect insurance money? All those well-crafted timbers lying forlorn and scorched in the parking lot? The stashed stack of Hites bubbling in cooked cans? A cook without a kitchen?

He sobbed. Then he spoke, slurring his words. That's right. I'm lost. Lost my job. Lost my friend. He gave up. James did. We used to talk together about how we'd do it. I always said I'd leave the engine running in the garage and hotbox my car, go out like a doped-up king. He always dreamed about that final day but could never decide which way he wanted to go. A gunshot's the quickest way, but he didn't have the heart to make someone else mop up his strewn-about brains from the kitchen floor. He was like that. Always considering others. Whenever I got depressed when we lived together, he'd always put down everything he had going on, and he had a lot of his own shit, to take care of me and make sure I was okay. We'd talk and chain-smoke cigarettes and eat sweet potato hashes and quiches on our doorsteps because we didn't have a dining room table or chairs yet, drinking orange juice and beers before we went to sleep in the early morning. Even after I moved away and got the job at Jimbo's, it always gave me hope that I could go on because I knew that James persevered going through the same bullshit too. But now he's gone. And Jimbo's is gone. I'm at the crossroads again. And I fucking hate crossroads.

Damn, this guy's life was depressing. I might have also killed myself if I was his friend. I refocused, trying to fathom why he kept persevering despite his pain.

Last time I came to a crossroad I moved here because James and I got into a fight. I've been getting into a groove keeping myself moving on the highways of the kitchen life, and I thought James must've also been doing well keeping himself on his own road. We started talking again recently and he told me that things were going well. He was starting a family. And do you know how he did it? He did it my way. I should've never put the idea in his head. You know about coupling? I learned about it in college before I dropped out. It's the idea that certain acts are tied to specific means. They only happen if those means are available. Me, I don't have a garage, and now I barely even have a functioning car, so I could never kill myself because I'd never use a rope or anything else. Well, he did it in the garage. In the new house he just started renting. With the headlights flashing. Only he didn't smoke up like I would've; he was coked out. Must've been jittering along with the music in his car, his dancing slowing down as his body succumbed to the carbon monoxide, but his brain running sprints along the dashboard doing laps endlessly until he finally collapsed, with his body still jerking around even after he passed out. His fiancé found him. She was holding their newborn. That's it, the kid's fatherless. He'll grow up depressed like me and his father.

Aaron. I can tell you're upset. It's okay. It's okay to be upset. Sometimes, the world sucks. We're going to figure this thing out together. Aaron, do you recognize my voice? Can you tell who you're talking to?

Sure, I'm talking to a Hotline Helper. I need your help, sir.

I am here to help you. But Aaron, you're not simply talking to some guy on the other end of the phone. Son, you're talking to your father.

How do you know about my father?

It's me, son. I'm on the phone here in Seoul.

He let out a drunken sob. Dad? Dad! Dad, I'm drinking a Hite, dad. Is that really you? You used to work there. You told me you helped them brew the beer even though mom said you were just a janitor there. Dad, why didn't you come pick me up from Mi-Sook's? She's dead now. Tell me why I shouldn't go and join her and James. Dad! Tell me something, tell me you'll see me! Let me come visit you. Please!

I took a deep sip from my coffee mug and let the coffee warm me up a bit. Straightened the calendar on my desk. Looked at the windows projecting euphoric beaded dancers dancing ecstatically all night long into a pink Tequila Sunrise.

Son, I'm here for you. You probably don't trust me, but you must. You know why I had to do what I did. Neither of us had a choice. You understand that, right?

I do, Dad. It's okay.

I'm sorry Aaron, but I have to give you the harsh truth. I never told you it because I knew you weren't ready. You may still not be ready, but we can't keep playing this game. You've got to man up and face the truth. It'll help you move on and do what you have to do.

I am ready Dad. Tell me.

The dirty truth is that it was your fault. It wasn't really, but it was. You couldn't have done anything about it. Your mom and I were responsible for what we did. We could afford to have your sister; we were in a good place. But then you came unexpectedly when I lost my job at Hite and your mother had to stay home with you and it was the off-season; no one was hiring. We couldn't make it work. Your mother went back home to her mother, and your sister had to grow up without her father. Let me ask you something. Son, what keeps you going? Why do you keep suffering needlessly?

I don't know, Dad. I guess I was hoping I'd figure that out when we talked.

Son, no one can give you those answers. They have to come from within. If you can't find them for yourself, then that should tell you something. Aaron, you didn't choose this burden to bear. The world handed it down to you. You have the power to shape your own destiny. You can cast off your yoke. I know you can see the path laid before you. Your whole life you've been following the paths laid out for you, terrified of coming to a T and having to decide left or right. This is your T, Aaron. And there's only one way to turn. Turn away from the suffering, Aaron. Relieve us of this pain. We don't have to live with it. Take the wheel, Aaron and hold on to it forever.

Okay, Dad, I will. I'd follow any advice you gave me.

You know, I'm glad we could finally have this talk. I feel a lot better. I hope you do too. The pain will soon lift up out of you. Turn off of your flooding highway. A comforting frozen driveway awaits. Goodbye, son.

Click. I smiled, knowing I'd helped another person solve his troubles.

After helping some more callers solve their troubles, I packed up my things and headed out to meet Chava for a night of drunken debauchery.

CHAPTER FIVE

Another morning. Another funeral. In another cemetery. Which meant I'd spared another life needless suffering. My rabbis told me when I was young that if you could save even a single life, it was as if you had saved the whole world.

The sun shone graciously. I walked through the cemetery's welcoming gates. Snow sat atop the tombstones, lending a beautiful shine to the scene.

Another sobbing mother stood by a pit with her daughter. Only these two and the preacher came. Broken hearts mourning together but alone. My boots started to lead me in their direction to offer a shoulder to lean on. A body to hug.

But I couldn't implicate myself; I had to avoid setting those crazed minds on the gears of conspiracy to find a first-degree killer when, in the end, Aaron had decided on his death voluntarily. And he'd made the right choice. And, don't be mistaken, it was indeed his choice.

I passed them. They stood forlorn, each submerged in his own agony. The preacher who couldn't find the right words to appease an impossible

motherly pain. The confused sister refusing to let
memories of all the times she bullied Aaron seep into
her conscience. The broken mother, wishing a husband
would hold her close, whispering soothing words into
her deaf ears.

I turned off to find an adjoining grave with a
Jewish star on it: Goldschmidt. I stooped down,
scooped up a stone, and placed it with others on the
slab sheltering Goldy's bones.

I looked back over a jacketed shoulder at the sad
scene, then pushed through the gates once more. Well,
there was another soul saved from his miseries. There
were plenty of other aching souls out there that needed
saving.

The sun set early. Chava joined me to meander the
neighborhood adorned with twinkling lights.

It was Christmas Eve. Parents and children
gathered in a line waiting to sit on Santa's lap. They
asked for Lego sets, giraffes, toy Mustangs,
PlayStations, iPhones and one good year from the
Timberwolves. Just one fucking series win in the
playoffs, that's all they desired. They were going on 14
damn years since they'd made it past the first round.

I took a deep breath. I'd promised myself I
wouldn't get so worked up over the team anymore.

But I did love basketball. Sports were the last
vestige of man's wars, the one way a person could still
prove his superiority over another. And even though it
didn't really matter whether you won or lost, because

the agony of defeat and the thrill of victory would all fade in the long stretch of time, for the briefest of moments, sports made it seem like our conquests mattered and that our skills and work and effort actually amounted to something. Of course, win or lose, when you walk out of the stadium and look around at the icy streets and cold people around you, you remember it's just a silly ballgame, exactly like the rest of life, and that none of it truly matters.

One more deep breath and I returned to the world. The kids played. The lights twinkled. Chava held my hand. We continued on down the street, enjoying the light display.

A sharply dressed man sat on a bench taking a swig from a bottle with a brown paper bag wrapped around it. His freshly ironed navy suit pants stood out beneath his winter coat.

The bench was large enough for three. Chava sat on the end of the bench, while I sat beside the man. He looked off into the hazy, sparkling night.

I looked back his way. How's it going?

Fine.

You had enough of your kids dragging you to each of the houses?

He grunted.

You have a family?

Yup.

Where are they?

Belgium.

Belgium? What're they doing there?

Living.

And what're you doing here?

Living.

Well, why the distance?

There was a faraway look in his eyes. A story played out in the ruins of his pupils. A man who never thought the love bug would bite him. He never imagined watching a woman walk down the aisle for him. Not after his heart was broken one too many times.

But she had found him. And they worked through some early struggles and cold feet to persevere in their blossoming love and give themselves entirely to each other until the end of time.

A glimpse of destiny. A young wife easing her loving husband inside her. Thunder crashing down from festive applauding heavens. Hugging and dancing joyously, an upraised arm hoisting a pregnancy test.

A woman swimming early in the morning and drinking power smoothies on the way to work. A small pain. Everything is fine. Another stab. It'll be okay. A woman doing Pilates and eating chicken thighs for two. A trip to the emergency room. A slow drive home. An empty womb. Wait a little before you try again. Here, use this rubber in the meantime. Hold each other close. Wallow together. Embrace.

It works. Time heals all wounds. Try again. This works too. A baby is born. A happy family. Don't have to worry about attaining that dream anymore.

The wife's cooking at home, one hand holding a

toddler on her hip, while the other hand flips some burgers in the skillet. Dad's coming home late, work's gotten serious. The strain of a non-profit. Long hours. Low pay. Ladders to climb. Asses to kiss.

Finally drive home. Another kid's born. He's asleep beside his brother. Dinner's on the table. Throw it in the microwave. Kiss the dreaming wife.

Climb out of bed to hit the gym at five. Shower quick. Throw on the suit. Rush to work. Get a coffee from the intern. Peek at the peaceful children. Kiss the wife's forehead while she sleeps.

Keep climbing the ladder. Reach the top. Wear fancy suits in the upstairs office, looking out on your empire of altruism. Enable people to help other people. Try and generate funds so you can pay them a decent wage. Go to meetings and then some more meetings. Grab a coffee. Buy a Tesla. Bask in the journalists' praises. Buy a Rolex. Might as well enjoy it. Glance at the framed picture of you, the wife and kids in the pumpkin field. Run off to another meeting.

Office Christmas party. Babysitter at home until midnight. Mom and Dad dance. Slacken the tie. Drink some cocktails. Let loose. Haven't had a time like this in a while. The babysitter calls. Jordan's thrown up. Don't worry. Mom rushes home to take care of the kid. Have a good time.

A drunk coworker spills her drink on those ironed pants. She helps clean them in the bathroom. A furtive glance. Stumble into a kiss. Confusion. Bra opened like a treasure chest. Forget everything. See the gold. Enjoy its shine. It's been earned. Come home. Collapse into bed. Sorry for waking you up, hon. How's Jordan?

The passion relents. Glances avoided. Eyes not met. How long does it last? A week? Surely not a month. She's a sharp one. That's why you fell in love with her. She goes back to her mom in Belgium and takes the kids with her. She never liked it here anyway. It's not too late for the kids to learn another language. They'll be better off there. Right?

His mouth couldn't relate this story, but I gathered it as he looked at me with eyes begging for help. My heart went out to him.

You think that bottle's gonna help you?

He shrugged. Nothing else has.

Chava stood up and offered him her hand. Come on, let's go get you a coffee.

A food truck was set up well to capitalize on the throngs of families. It sold hot chocolate with whipped cream for the kids and coffee and spiked cider for the adults.

We strolled down the middle of the street with people frolicking on both sides. Lights of red and green and baby Jesuses and eight-foot-tall wrapped present boxes and sleighs on roofs and train sets running around and around, endlessly chasing unreachable cabooses, and a warm yet frigid night full of laughter and moonlit walks and revelry.

The man was ready to speak, having drank some soul-warming coffee.

You see, it was just that one little mistake I made.

But there are no second chances in this world.

It's going to be okay, sir. You'll see your kids. I'm sure they're doing fine. They're learning new languages, seeing the world. They're doing good. It might seem like they don't need you. But they remember you. I'm sure you framed a picture of yourself with the kids for them to put on their bedside tables, right? So they can look at you and hug you when they miss you?

The man shrugged and walked off.

Chava looked at him. He must be the saddest man I've ever met.

You think he needs my help?

She nodded, so I chased him down. Hey, sir. I'm actually a trained professional. I can help you out. I work at the Happy Hotline. Here's my card. If you're ever feeling so down that you can't imagine making it to tomorrow, give me a call. Don't mention it. Get some sleep. Things will be better in the morning. It's the holidays. Smile.

CHAPTER SIX

Chava waited for me to return to bed, all splayed out like a starfish. The aroma of our lust lingered in the air. Snow fell outside. It was Christmas morning.

You should probably go and pee too.

First come back to bed.

I'm gonna go smoke a cigarette. Is the porch okay?

You're no fun. Chava stretched out languorously. Sure. I'll have one too.

The sun rose over the apartment complex. In each of the apartments families undertook that classic American dance. The children unwrapped presents, the parents feigned shock at what Santa delivered, the children jumped into the arms of their parents and then jumped right back down to build, install, form, play, and get up to regular child shenanigans. The parents smiled, knowing their paychecks were spent well. They headed to the kitchen to kiss and hug and laugh and look deep into each other's eyes and get breakfast going.

It was a beautiful day. The snow fell as if out of a postcard. But fuck it was cold out.

There's nothing worse than smoking in the winter.

It's nothing like smoking in the summer, when you can lounge around with a loose body, slackened shoulders, indifferent fingers. You don't have to pass the cigarette back and forth between your hands while the empty hand grabs whatever warmth it can find in the heat of the groin. Shit, I can't even remember what summer's like. Gotta escape this town for good. Don't know how I've lived here my whole life. Gotta find somewhere else. Somewhere less depressingly cold.

Oh, yeah. I got sidetracked by the fucking cold.

The people were celebrating Christmas. The families. The roommates. They got gifts for each other. Small kind things. Little thoughtful things. Even the lonely people, living in a building full of couples and families and friends, were, for the moment, happy. They lit themselves pumpkin-spiced candles, brewed some coffee, cut themselves a nice slice of apple pie to go with a dollop of ice cream, and called home. They opened presents from the mail, smiling. Tomorrow would be a completely different story.

Chava sidled up to me on the porch, wearing only a robe. You got a cigarette for me? God, I love Christmas.

You do? Here, take mine; I'll light another one.

Thanks. Of course; it's Christmas.

But you're Jewish.

So are you. But that doesn't mean we can't love Christmas.

But aren't you religious?

You still think that after what I let you do to me

last night?

Her naughty eyes made me blush. I don't know. I just assumed you were because you have a Hebrew name. It's Chava, not Eve. And your ex's name was Yossi. Seems like you all come from religious families. Me, I'm just Jay. My mom raised me as best as she could on the religion, but by the time I had my bar mitzvah, I realized she was just using it to trick herself into believing that her life had meaning. She was silly. She'd drive through five green lights in a row and would say God was looking out for her. Me, well I never needed anyone but myself looking out for me. Especially after her God took her away when I was 14. Little good all those prayers did for her. Either way though, we definitely never celebrated Christmas.

Oh. Well, I was also raised religious. We used to go to the synagogue every Shabbat. We didn't *really* celebrate Christmas. But I always loved it. Growing up in the Iron Range, there weren't that many Jews around. There was only one synagogue in town. When December came, all the lights would go up and everybody adopted a festive mood. You'd walk around at night and it would be freezing, colder than hell, but everyone was so nice. We'd walk into any of our neighbors' houses and they'd make us a nice cup of hot chocolate and we'd gossip and talk and watch movies and have snowball fights with all our friends. And when Christmas came, the Andersons, our neighbors, would invite my sisters and me over and they'd give us each a little gift and we'd unwrap it with everyone else under the Christmas tree. It was so beautiful. The Andersons and Hansons and Olsons would come over on the first night of Hannukah and we'd give them presents, too, and spin the dreidels and eat latkes. I miss it up there. No one's left now, though. All the jobs are down here in the cities. The synagogue had to close. Not that I'd go to it now, anyways.

A Jew who loves Christmas. Strange. We killed the poor man.

Very funny. You know, I wish you'd have gotten me something.

Well, shit. I assumed you didn't do Christmas. I could get you a Hannukah gift, there's still a few days left of that, right? But hey, why didn't you get me something?

I didn't know if you celebrated any of the holidays.

Well, I might just have to get you something. Do you have an ashtray?

Yup, I'll go grab it.

The phone rang. It had to be the philandering businessman. That was quick. I put him on speaker.

How's it going, sir?

Not good. I can't keep going on like this, seeing all these happy families celebrating the holidays while I'm stuck here, all alone.

Well, Mr. Kundin, it seems like sleeping with your coworker was the wrong decision.

Chava returned with the ashtray and I put out the cigarette. The sad man on the phone kept talking as I peeked at Chava's breasts underneath her loose robe.

You know, Jay, I'm tired of apologizing for that. Julie knows I'm sorry. I promised her I'd do anything to make things right with her. But she was on the first plane out and never gave me a chance. That was her decision, not mine.

I ran my hand down Chava's torso, parting her robe. What's wrong, Mr. Kundin? You miss your kids?

Yes, I miss them. We used to buy them presents each night of Hannukah and we'd light the candles and spin the dreidels. They were so excited and happy, they used to jump around and sing these silly, made up songs. Without them, the house is so big and empty and quiet. I need those moments back in my life. Life's worthless without them. Work's meaningless. The job's okay; it's fine. But I used to work so hard to make sure we could get our kids nice presents. When the holidays came, it would all be worth it, all the hard work. Julie was so happy, and the kids were over the moon. There's no joy in any of it now.

I was having a hard time concentrating on what he was saying. Well, then why do you keep working?

Honestly, I don't know. The money piles up in my bank account, but there's no one to spend it on. You know, she won't even let me pay her alimony, so I can at least feel like I'm helping taking care of the kids. Her parents are in the diamond business over there and take care of her. So, the bank account's full, but the house is empty when I get home and it's all worth nothing. You know what I'm saying?

Chava's body was begging me to wrap up the call.

Yes, Mr. Kundin, I know exactly what you're saying. I'll tell you what, I'll give you a little holiday miracle. It seems like you miss feeling like your life's worth something, right? And that you used to get that feeling by sharing gifts with others. So, how about we do a little Hannukah gift swap? I'll get you a nice little present and you can also get me something, if you want. We can meet up at Lake Bde Maka Ska later. Oh, and Mr. Kundin? You can make it a surprise, but just so you know, I am pretty fond of watches. All right, Mr. Kundin. I'll see you at five. Happy Hannukah. Click.

Chava snuggled up to me. That's a smart trick you played, hinting about a watch.

You like that, huh?

Mm. Kinda turns me on.

Oh, is that so? Well, why don't we go do something about it?

CHAPTER SEVEN

Lake Bde Maka Ska was frozen. Couples walked hand in hand around its shore. Plumes of smoke seeped out from tall chimneys, but otherwise, the sky was blue.

I carried the perfect Secret Santa present in my hand, cradling it beneath my armpit. It contained something that would forever enhance Mr. Kundin's life and assist him in finding an escape to a better place.

He gave me an awkward hug in greeting. Hi Jay. I got you something. I hope you like it. I didn't get you a Rolex or anything too over the top, but I hope you like what I picked out.

He handed me the wrapped present. There's a special delight you get when waiting for someone to open a present you got them. Parents appreciate this special moment more than anyone else because it's been so long since they received a present that truly excited them. Even if their spouse does get them something good, the recipient is still often paying for it in the end. So, giving presents is the only joy left to them when it comes to gifts.

Oh, wow! Check it out! A black Fossil watch. You

know, you don't know me at all, but I always liked watches like this one with a couple of dials on them. Something about them always did it for me. Thanks so much, Mr. Kundin. That's a really great present. Hey, I got something for you too.

Mr. Kundin smiled a hesitant smile. He didn't need anything. He'd filled up his house with as many things as he could. He kept going back to Home Depot and Best Buy, buying every tool and gadget he could think of to keep himself busy, deplete his savings a little and fill up his cavernous house. And, of course, to forget his sins and their cost.

He opened the box, which contained a beaming light.

Mr. Kundin, are you familiar with the Jewish tradition of the *ner tamid*, the everlasting flame?

I've heard of it.

He pulled the electric candle out from the box and turned it over in his hands, looking at it. The light glowed, as it always had, ever since it was manufactured. It didn't light itself and it didn't turn itself off, it simply glowed and continued to glow. It flickered faintly.

I continued on as he stared at the candle: You know, society, religion, God, they all tell us that life goes on forever and that you have to keep living it, no matter what, no matter how much you're suffering. But I'm giving you this electric candle, this eternal flame, and you know what? You have the power to take the batteries out just like that if you want to. There's

CHAPTER FOUR

The world conspires. It takes unrelated events and throws them at people, turning them over and over until they're a seeping ball of dust.

Rivers, streams and creeks spew forth from mountains. The rains come and the waters leak out of their homes, sweeping away people's poles and beams just when they're ready to set the purlins on their roofs. Only then do the waters recede.

Then winter comes and the water channels freeze over. Forest fires arrive on the shores, burning up and cracking well-set foundations. Spring thaws the earth and birds return from warmer lands. But the timber's gone and the homeless are assailed by infinite mosquitos.

Masterpieces are written that go unpublished. Friends console the author, offering hope that the big break will come tomorrow, but manuscripts burn. Lovers leave. Lonely and sad selves wait on the brink to overtake their jubilant counterparts when the clock strikes midnight.

Cities are sieged and then sacked. Fertile soils get salted and yield no more fruits. Rome falls. America nothing so simple. It doesn't have to be like they tell us it does.

I looked deep into his eyes, which looked confused, but hopeful. You control your own flame, Mr. Kundin. No one can force you to keep it burning against your will.

He nodded but just stood there, still unsure of what exactly he should do.

I don't have to tell you what this symbolizes, do I, Mr. Kundin? You're a smart and successful man. Go back to your empty house. Place the candle on your dining room table, or wherever. Contemplate the flame burning endlessly inside it. How long has your pain been burning inside you? Consuming you? It has consumed you. You are the flame, Mr. Kundin. You've been burning for so long, you forgot it wasn't you who lit the flame in the first place. The flame can't burn out on its own. It's been burning for far too long; it's forgotten what it's like not to burn. You can ease your own suffering. You don't have to live in an eternal winter, awaiting a spring that never comes. Give the fire a rest, Mr. Kundin. Can't you feel how tired it is?

I didn't go to his funeral. It would've been the same as Yossi's.

He really was Yossi. Rather, he was a different iteration of him, if only Yossi had lived a bit longer.

Indeed, Mr. Kundin's funeral would've been quite similar to Yossi's. Only, there would've been no one at the cemetery grieving for him.

CHAPTER EIGHT

It was a happy New Year's Eve. We were finally over the pre- and post-Christmas spikes. There were so many callers. So many souls to hand hold. It was good getting a break to forget all of them and enjoy a nice party.

I put on a star-filled blue vest over my naked torso, adorning my neck with a matching bowtie. Chava wore a dress with yellow stars that almost reached down to her knees. We clutched our arms around each other, trying to share some long-forgotten warmth on the brutal, 100-foot walk from the car to the house. Frostbite nearly set in.

We entered her friend's house to lights and laughter and music and drinks and love. Everyone was either happy or convincing themselves and each other of their happiness. I had my first midnight kiss to look forward to in a while.

Girls dancing on dining room tables lifted overflowing red cups. Impatient boys grabbed girlfriends' asses, trying to kiss juicy lips, but missed and caught turned cheeks. It seemed like everyone was having a ball. It was impossible not to get caught up in the revelry.

But lonely young men smoked outside or stood against walls, evading eyes. They scanned bookshelves seeking compelling tales of glory, or else bent down to tie tied shoelaces, or else oversmiled, hoisting a can of beer in the air and chugging it down through the crowd's eager countdown.

Oh, you thought I forgot about all of you? I didn't fail to see you hiding in the corner. I keep you all in my heart. Truly. I'd have kissed each one of you if I could have.

But then the clock struck midnight and Chava grabbed my vest with both hands, pulling my body to hers, and the new year came in with joyous drunk smooches. She took her late Christmas-Hannukah present and, opening the box with a squeal, hung the blue and yellow Jewish-star earrings from her ears.

She leaned in, stars jangling around her head, and passed a drunken whisper into my ear. She had a secret to share with me in the bathroom.

The bulb was expired. I stumbled in behind her, almost crashing into her and throwing her through the sink and mirror. But she caught me with her mouth, wet lips smooching, black roof spinning, embracing in the eternity of the warm closet of night. The tension escalated. The music and joy and laughter sang out from the party. My fingers slipped beneath her short dress finding heaven, but no, she slid down vigorously, taking me, singing those highest of notes, imbibing the sweetest of liquors, cascading all feeling down from brain to brain, attaining pure and drunken bathroom world joy, finding an everlasting ascent up to the dark bulb, exploding it with light, until it terminated once more and all was dark again and calm.

I exited after sending her out first; shouldn't let them know what we were up to. Zip up, head out, they do know, they knew the second she stepped out first. Bathrooms are for blowjobs, her friends call out, so raise a cup, it's a party, life itself is a party, so enjoy it while you can.

But in the corner sat a broken boy, alone, holding a full beer, not lifting his cup. I sauntered over to him.

Hey there, bud. Something wrong?

No, nothing. I'm fine. It doesn't matter. You wouldn't care.

No, I do. I really do care. Please, tell me.

I was completely genuine this time. Don't know what got into me. Maybe it was some kind of post-orgasm cheerfulness.

Festive music played while he talked. Well, you know how it is, man. I had a girl. Things went south. That was like a year and a half ago. Then I lost my job and got really depressed. I thought about ending it but then a kind stranger helped me, and I was able to turn things around. But then I saw on Facebook that my ex-girlfriend got engaged. And here I am. I've barely caught a warm glance in the eyes of someone since we broke up. So, I guess I'm kind of feeling hopeless again.

Joseph, is that you? It's me, Jay. I'm the one you called at the Hotline. Wow, what a small world.

He glanced into my eyes before returning his gaze to the floor. Wow, yeah. Hey, thanks for helping me out then. Sorry I'm not doing so well now.

Oh, you don't have to be sorry. So, what happened, you got a job?

No, not exactly, but you did inspire me to turn things around and start taking better care of myself. I actually did get to a pretty good place and started working on my novels full-time. I always wanted to be a writer. But I've been writing this really dark novel. I think at first it was helping me to process my emotions, but lately it feels like I've been falling into the darkness that I'm writing about. And then just the other day I discovered that my ex-girlfriend got engaged and it kind of broke me.

Hey, well, good for you, Joseph. I'm glad you found something worthwhile to pursue. And I feel you on hearing the news. It's definitely tough. But here's the advice I'll give you, Joseph: It's all about the narratives we tell ourselves. You gotta put yourself in the position of yourself when you're 75. What's the story you're telling? You're going to tell the story of a young man who had his heart broken. There's going to be that period of loneliness and longing. But you know how the story's going to continue, right? This is your growth phase. You're finding yourself; you're learning about the world, you're understanding what it takes to be a man, you're making yourself desirable. You're following your dream of becoming a writer. And your woman of a lifetime is on her way and she's going to find you one day soon, and when she does, you'll live happily together forever. You'll tell your grandkids about the time when you lost all hope, but then you bore down and really got ahold of yourself, and everything worked out fine in the end. And those few short months or years when you were alone before you found her are going to seem so silly in retrospect. You were waiting to be in the perfect place at the perfect time to find each other. And you will. So, chin up, cowboy. She'll come when the time's right. You'll be okay, Joseph; you'll be okay.

I patted Joseph on the head and myself on the back. I did my job, put in some overtime. Mr. Joy would be proud.

It was good to pull someone back from the brink. It reminded me how truly useless it all was, these suckers' desperate, sad strivings. Some people just weren't meant to be happy, and they only made it harder on themselves when they put so much pressure on attaining happiness. The only escape from this trap of a cycle was for someone else to show them how futile their struggles really were. I would truly, genuinely help the next person I saw so upset. I'd give them the advice they had to hear, not the encouragement they wanted to hear.

I went to find that sexy lady draped in stars and watched her dance, one hand holding a drink, the other soaring and skipping about in the air, legs kicking in rhythm, feet dancing in step. I strode up to her and squeezed her cute ass.

Having a good time?
Great! You wanna get out of here?

Back at her place. Easing her into bed, slowly pulling off her star dress, kissing up and down her neck, sucking on her breasts, returning to embrace her mouth, pouring all my love down into it; take it, it's yours, it's all yours; my body is yours.

Sliding down her navel and legs, kissing and licking her wetness, looking up at her head thrown back in ecstatic release, her mouth open, forgetting to breathe for the pleasure, moaning loudly, loudly, loudly, finally spasms sprint up from her legs to her breasts to her beautiful head. I climb north, caressing her soft brown hair, holding her close, interlocking fingers, hands stretching upward, and take her slowly, luxuriating in her sweaty womanly scent.

We become one. We become the world, the light, the joy. It lasts forever, and forever goes slower, slower, it lingers, we kiss slowly, kiss deeply, I want her to wrap her legs around my back enclosing us in a tomb of delight, but she doesn't, but no matter; she lays there mysteriously, looking into my eyes, which are full of joy, as I hold onto her hands tightly, still going slow but pulling back to look at her, fully appreciate her, seeing her as if for the first time. Her soul opens up to me. I've never truly seen her before, but suddenly here she is, she's the one, the light, then we are the light; I see her cute, chubby face as a child, see her older sisters bullying her and see her retreating into the solace of her room, where she plays with her dolls until she grows up to care for the Earth, for the people, for the animals, for the plants, for every living thing, and she scoops up cigarettes from dirty beaches, composts her shit, pets stray cats, massages her mom's aching back, cooks veggie burgers for her dad, looks up at the stars on warm, hopeful nights, loves life, reveres it above all else, and, finally, wears lab coats and stethoscopes and studies medicine to care for her fellow man. She's patient, and she takes it slow, and slow, and slow, it rises, it grows, love, love, love, oh, Chava.

She drew a deep breath as I pulled out, letting the overflowing rubber sit on its pulsating pedestal. I looked into her green eyes. They were searching, looking for something. She shut her eyes. I hoped she'd found whatever she was looking for.

A song played from her phone. The music was slow and sad. Her head rested far away. Her face was questioning. Then it gave up. Another sad song played.

What's this song, Chava? It's making me sad.

I'm sad.

What? Why are you sad?

Something's changed. I don't know. But I can feel it in my gut.

Maybe that's the sex talking.

No, it's deeper than that. It's different. Look, I'm going back to school in Tucson next week. It wasn't going to work out anyway.

What? I could come to Tucson. The Hotline has a branch there. I'd love to come to the desert and escape the Minnesota cold. I'd be glad to. We have something, we can't just give up on it.

I'm sorry, but I can't do that. The same thing happened with Yossi. He wanted more from me than I could give him. He gave me his soul and he wanted mine, but I could barely give him my heart. I just felt the same thing. It's not like at the cemetery. There, we were close. There was a raw animal passion to it. But now I can see that you've fallen for me and I just can't play that game. Not again. I'm really sorry. Maybe it's for the best that we end it now before I disappoint you. You deserve more than me. You're a good man. You care about people.

What? I don't deserve more than you. I deserve you. I want you. I need you.

No, I can tell. I've been trying to trust my gut more and I have to listen to it now. It's telling me that we're not meant to be. I'm really sorry. It's better that I tell you now than lead you on and have you move and follow me to the desert and then when it doesn't work out there, you'll be stranded with the dust and the rocks, all alone, not knowing how you got there. I've played that game before. It's no fun for anyone. It's for the best. I'm sorry. I think you should go.

The world twisted and turned, shuttling me along in its orbit.

Feet carried body into the bathroom, hand dropped wasted seed into the trashcan beside the toilet. Vest covered torso, bag jumped into hand and head turned around from behind the wheel of the car to glance back at her standing by the curb. Shivering hands grabbed the wheel.

The car crept off slowly, hand waved in the rearview mirror, eyes turned back and glimpsed her standing there, the car drove on, her body diminished in the driver's side mirror, the car drove on, head turned back over shoulder searching for her but she was gone, and head forced its way forward to face the road and the car drove on into the night.

CHAPTER EIGHT

Back out into the icy empty world.

I walked down muddy melted oozing paths by the lonely lake. It was too cold for anyone else to be out today. Only someone as crazy and cold and miserable and disgusted by the world as me would venture into its most tormenting brutal form to willingly embrace it.

The happy ones would appear to dance and skip when the world offered sunshine and warmth. The satisfied ones would run all bundled up from home to car to office and pull the shades up as soon as the engineers of day bridged the vast unpleasant chasm of night. But only the depraved and destructive ones would emerge when it was minus-20 degrees with the windchill and also sunless, a perfect day for wallowing and coming to grips with bitter realities.

I couldn't succumb to those Wim Hof delusions and try to trick my body that everything was really all right in the world, that the thermometer was a sham, that you could breathe deeply five times and exhale vigorously seven times for seven seconds a pop until your heartbeat stabilized, balancing and counterbalancing you on a perfectly aligned plane of warm coziness. Breathe in once, exhale once. Then twice, then thrice. Breathe, forget to breathe, exhale, inhale, whatever the fuck — mouth nose brain lungs it doesn't matter, it goes in once upon excretion from the womb and goes out once upon final, glorious descent from the prison of the ceaseless compulsory in-out flow to the place where no innate being forces you to breathe anymore and all is utter freedom.

No. Don't succumb. Let the wind circle and envelop you. Let it snake around the body like a chilled, weighted blanket, forcing all your thoughts to its beacon, trapping your tongue stuck to its pole.

But then I looked up from the mud to see a woman out on the lake. It seemed like she was disrobing, opening herself up to the cold even as the wind stabbed and bit my neck, the only part of my body not bundled up.

I approached her and saw that she was looking down through an open window of the frozen abyss, pulling her mink coat back over her bare shoulders. Wool-coated leather moccasins guarded her feet from the bite of the thick ice.

Say, lady, what are you doing there? Trying to tempt the fish to jump up out of the lake with your boobs?

No, silly. I'm performing the final ritual in my sacred body before I experience my last immersive pleasure. This form, this Josephine, has given me great joy, every single one of the joys on the list. I've done them all, except for one. So, now it's my time.

Let me get this straight, are you saying that you're going to jump into the freezing water and that there's going to be some innate, intense pleasure in it? That doesn't sound right to me.

Oh, but it'll be such a distinct pleasure. You breathe in and out and align your body and mind and then submerge and experience the fullness and totality of the cold. At first, the cold shocks you with a million tiny water bubbles swarming and crashing down on every inch of your body, but then you ride the wave and experience the ultimate serenity of the Earth's winter. First, you jump and your toes touch the surface of the water and your feet feel the cool clasp of the lake. Then, the chill rises up the legs to the groin, up past the hips to the breasts, and finally the water overcomes the mouth, nose, ears, eyes and the last strand of hair submerges, and then the shock dissipates and the cold water seeps into the mouth and funnels down, invigorating the throat, the chest, the lungs, down to the stomach, the bladder, then finally down through the urethra as the water finishes its cycle, releasing into the ready clasp of its brother water molecules, and I become the water and the water is the water and the pee is the water and it's all the soul and life and elixir of the world. And the full release and acceptance of the cold into my body means that my body will give its cold pulse right back to the lake and then everything will become one. And then I can move on to my next form.

I was in shock at this madwoman and shook my

head, partly to get my blood moving again and partly to try and understand her. Wow. I can't say I could've ever imagined that experience from your perspective. So, if this is the last pleasure you're after, what are the other pleasures you've done so far? I can't even imagine what kind of stuff you've tried if this is your idea of a good time.

She intermittently robed and disrobed as she breathed deeply, revealing a scarred and lovely body submitted to all the excitements and brutalities on sale in the markets of human desire.

Well, I've jumped out of a bunch of planes, one on every continent. There's this great thrill you get when you're hovering above it all in your own atmosphere, with only the birds and clouds for company, you know? Let's see, what else? I swam naked with sharks, touching their fins as they passed under me, the raw fear pumping through every vein in my body. I ran an ultramarathon barefoot in the Mojave Desert, tearing my soles clean off my feet. I slept with Clooney; he's a gracious lover who really knows what he's doing; I felt like I was bathing in a vast cloud of exploding marshmallows while he made love to me. I also slept with Barbra Streisand and Ice Cube; one was submissive and really let me take all the power I wanted and feel the sheer thrill of domination, the other was pretty brutal and allowed me that rare delicacy of pure vulnerability and capitulation. I'll let you guess who was who. I wrote and acted in a play off-Broadway; there's something about the thrill of being naked and baring your body and soul in front of a crowd of people, you know? I danced to bagpipes in the hot desert on shrooms and acid at Burning Man as the glow of the sun engulfed my twisting ecstatic blazing form; I ran with the bulls in Pamplona but was so zonked on painkillers from an accident while bungee jumping in New Zealand that I barely remember diving out of the way of the charging bulls. I've experienced rainforests and deserts and tundra and marshes and beaches and cliffs and the open ocean and lakes and ponds and rivers and streams and creeks and brooks the width of your thumb and metropolises and cities and towns and villages and remote rural outposts; I don't know, man. All I can say is I've lived. I've fucked, been fucked, flew, soared, skipped, crawled, hiked, drank, smoked, injected, popped, ran, swam, bathed, had my heart broken, broken hearts, luxuriated, wallowed, basked, burned, and now I will freeze.

Sounds like a wild life.

Yup. And my next form will be good to me too. I wouldn't quite say I'm excited for it, because you have to appreciate every form for what it is, and if I was too anxious for my next form that I left this form too early, then I wouldn't deserve my next form but would instead end up being a rock destined to sit and wait in place forever, which would be fine too, because every form is special for what it is, but I do need to accept this form for what it is and only leave it at exactly the right time, because the timing's of immense

importance. And then my soul will become the cold
and will remain in the water and float around until it
finds the belly of a big musky fish and it'll seep into
one of the sperm inside the fish and then I'll be passed
on from daddy musky to the eggs that mommy musky
has laid and I'll go through the whole life cycle and be
a massive musky swimming under the ice in the winter
and up to the surface to tease the fishermen in the
summer and then I'll eventually get caught and eaten
and I'll pass through the digestive system of a young
boy and go out his bowels into his outhouse and his
grandpa will use the waste for fertilizer for his garden
and I'll enter the vines there and pass into one of the
seeds of a tomato and he'll take a few bites from the
tomato but it won't be ripe yet so he'll throw me and
all my seed brothers into the forest where a blue jay will
eat the tomato and I'll pass through the digestive tract
of the jay and lie on the forest floor until a squirrel eats
me along with a pine nut she was really after and then
I'll be the egg in the squirrel's ovary and a seed will
come to join me after a night of beautiful squirrel
passion and we'll be one and be born in the spring and
then we'll be the split soul of a beautiful, tormented
flying squirrel and leap and soar through the trees and
save nuts for winter and have a good time getting fat
in the summer and it'll be a tough life but probably my
favorite life.

I shook my head again. Those are a ton of very
bold presumptions about all kinds of different lives.
You make it seem like it's all inevitable. How could you

possibly be so sure of your fate? What happens when you just die and none of that comes true?

I don't know. I'm just sure. I guess remembering all of my past lives helps. They linger in my dreams and I get to relive them almost every night. What about you, though? You seem pretty skeptical and negative. Maybe you're just upset and that's not who you usually are. I don't know, but your aura has something hungry and desperate in it, like it's seeking an escape. What's keeping you from escaping down that road you know you need to travel? No, don't tell me the answer. You gotta figure that out for yourself. I've got my own lives to experience.

She disrobed, removed her moccasins and raised her head to bask in the glow of the sun, which peeked out from behind the clouds. Then she cannonballed into the frozen waters. The splash soaked my pants and my legs shook as I walked across the frozen lake to the shore.

Maybe she was onto something. Was I living my life right? Was I sure that the answers I'd found and been giving to those poor suffering souls were the right ones? Was I leading them off a cliff I wouldn't dare jump off myself?

No, no doubts. They were definitely better off because of my help. I could see their crushed faces smiling, blown-out brains freed from their prisons, overdosed stomachs permitted to cease their grueling work.

I guess the question was when to take the jump

myself. If only I could talk to Chava about it, I was sure she'd have a good answer. That or we could fuck each other's brains out and I could forget my existential malaise for a little bit.

I drank down a few quick beers at the corner bar and kept moving. I was actually enjoying the cold, which enveloped me pleasantly like the squirrel girl must have enjoyed her bath. Maybe she had it right, and it was best to embrace the cold for what it was.

I took my gloves off. Snow fell and lingered on my outstretched fingertips as my muffled footsteps plodded beneath me.

How would I know when I should end it all? I looked around me. There were many naked, sturdy branches jutting out all around. All I needed was a rope.

I stepped back onto the ice and looked down into the mirror of the lake, realizing from my unsteady reflection how drunk I was. I pulled out my phone and punched some numbers into it. Hey. I hope it's okay that I called you — I could hear myself slurring, but I kept talking — Well, um, I guess I just wanted to say that I don't really know if I should go on if none of it matters anyway, you know? I've been trying to figure out when's the best time, but it's impossible to say. If I helped other people, then why can't I help myself? You know? But whatever. You don't really care. It doesn't matter to you, either. You've played this game before and we know how it turns out for the other guy.

Jay, I do care. I didn't want that to happen to

Yossi. Are you okay?

Sure, I'm fine. I mean, does it matter if I'm okay or not? I could be having the best day of my life or the worst day, but either way, I'll still shit out of loose bowels when my last breath eases out of me, and you won't be beside me anyway to make my death feel like it matters, so who gives a fuck?

Jay, it's completely valid to feel that way. I know it's hard going through what you're going through, but you'll find someone else, someone who's right for you and who can love you the way you deserve to be loved.

Yeah, but what if that person ends up being you, but at a different point in life, so it's still you, but it's a different you, when you're finally ready to be in a relationship? So, I can't go off and find someone else, only for you to finally be ready when I'm unavailable. I'd be stuck in a worthless relationship and miserable and I'd eventually leave her for you anyway, when it's finally a different but a ready you, but then you'd be overcome by the burden of having me give up everything for you. But something would be off like it wasn't before, when everything was good. So, I'll stay single for now and wait for you and you can take your time and when you're ready and have your life sorted out and the timing's right we'll get back together and everything will be fine.

Jay, I tried to make it clear to you that we were done, but I understand that it's taken some time for you to fully process it. It wouldn't be fair to me or you or us to lead you on like that and have you think that one day it will all be fine and we'll be in love and everything will go on happily ever after. I'd be lying to myself and to you. It's probably for the best for us not to talk from now on. There are other girls out there, Jay. We weren't even together for that long. Don't repeat that same cliché again. Just move on.

The phone clicked off.

Fuck it. None of it mattered anyway. What she said didn't matter, I didn't matter, she didn't matter, the relationship didn't matter, it wouldn't matter if it kept going, and it didn't matter that it ended. It'd all lead to the same shit anyway.

My head spun. I walked and walked but felt like I wasn't getting anywhere as I strode into the teeth of the wind.

I kept walking for a while, not knowing whether I was moving or not. Then, I looked up and saw an island laying in the middle of the frozen Mississippi. A taunting ascent rose to a bluff overlooking the Twin Cities.

The island was its own universe, living between worlds, like Dante's Purgatory. It was a world of never-ending tests and travails and isolation. A world of sin without redemption. A world of endless life.

The island became for me everything, the center of the universe. Everyone lived on it, suffered on it, was stuck on it. And they were all forever seeking an ascent that never came, and a messiah who'd forgotten to return.

I walked on the ice around the island's crooked

shores in endless circles. Chava's words echoed over and over in my head.

Words and ideas and theories came to mind. I remembered hearing about a study that proved that couples in brightly lit observing rooms could be easily identified for success or failure. Scientists could discern whether couples would or would not enjoy long-lasting peace, harmony and love. They'd sit them down and listen to how they conversed with each other.

Look through the glass barrier into the viewing room. A hint of a misogynistic put-down? The relationship won't last. Nervous escalating disagreements indicating disrespect? Won't last. A smile and a thoughtful, considerate word? Check. Holding hands, looking into each other's eyes with understanding? Check. Respectful adherence to the wants and needs of the other? Check. And if the couple aces the test, they're destined to live together in love forever.

But fuck all that lab-room psychology. It assumes the world doesn't get in the way and break them up. It assumes that people actually want love in the first place. But clearly, they don't. Because things don't work out. The guy jumps off a bridge and the girl runs away to medical school to play with her cadavers. No sailing off into the sunset, leaving all your worries behind. The only thing you could always count on was the hollow island world.

The air was still and lifeless. The hardened ground crackled underfoot. A reedy plant, unrooted, sat on the snowy ground, waiting futilely to be replanted. A wooden canoe that long ago had been hauled up onto shore was buried under a mound of snow.

Ruminations floated in the dark clouds above. Too many people suffered yet. A rise in ambition was necessary. The hotline had many callers, but I could only talk to them one at a time. I needed to raise those numbers.

I headed back to the river's shore. Lust had gotten ahold of me. A deep understanding was thrown askew by a small and sweet glimpse of a different life. Convictions held deep in the pools of the soul were drained so quickly by that temptress of love. I needed to reset it all and remember what prompted those convictions in the first place.

A vision reappeared of the naked, suffering soul smiling on the ice beneath the bridge. I held his memory close. He was my messenger from above. Those kinds of visions only came maybe once in a decade, if you were lucky. I tried to hold onto him in my heart, to remember the release I had given him.

But the heart's only capable of holding onto its revelations for so long. Blood initially boils in the veins, but the feeling eventually fades to indifference as time passes. You have to drag those embers of feeling up from the heart into the durable chambers of the mind, so they won't rot.

I retreated from the island and walked back across the river, nodding to two ice fishermen drinking beers. They offered me one, which I graciously accepted, letting them feel good about passing on their joy to someone else. I moved on, cracking open the can.

I had to start the ball rolling again. I was onto a good thing before all this relationship shit threw me out of whack. I'd give the ball a strong push, kick it, spike it, send it flying, soar along with it. It was time to go to work and set the plan in motion. Then, maybe once I'd helped everyone who needed me, I could give myself the same sweet release I was giving to others.

CHAPTER EIGHT

I was heading back into work when Joseph attacked me with his cheerfulness.

Hey, it's you! The savior himself! I wanted to say thanks so much for what you said to me the other night. And for the other time when I called. I really wouldn't have survived without you.

Hey, Joseph. What are you doing here?

I just had a great hot yoga hug-therapy session. The instructor, Alberto, has really helped me see the world in a more balanced light. Hot yoga hug therapy's all about releasing your sweat and troubles from your body. Then, you have to release your revulsion at your own and everyone else's puddles of sweat and troubles, and then you can embrace them and yourself for who we all really are, deep down. Once we did that, we were all able to work together to try and improve ourselves.

Sounds lovely.

You sound skeptical, but it really was. Alberto's helped me understand that we have these parallel paths of happiness and satisfaction, where happiness is being with the people you love, and satisfaction is accomplishing your goals. We have to find the balance between them. If we can, we'll find that we're teetering on this thin ledge between happiness and satisfaction, doing our best to find meaning in the middle path. Once the path is established, though, even if it's super thin, we can expand it until it gets big enough that we're not at risk of falling off the path anymore. It's really helped me a lot to see the world this way. It gives me focus, you know?

Oh, for sure, sounds terrific. Hey, you know, I've been thinking about our talk the other night. I realized that I gave you the wrong message, probably because I was overly cheery from all the booze we were drinking. You know, it is about narratives, like I said. But I was deluding you that your narrative would automatically turn out how you want it to turn out. The truth is that life's not a romantic novel. It's full of bitter twists and turns and oftentimes it ends in the middle of the book. And, unfortunately, the page it ends on is usually an unhappy one.

Well, I think that I both agree and disagree with you, Jay. You're right that life is a story. It's told on the pages of the soul. All the words are already written there, and they reveal themselves to us as we pass through the chapters of time. But I believe that the stories are good ones. I really do.

But you're assuming that the storyteller isn't some drunk fool writing in a language he doesn't even know. Or, maybe he does know what he's writing, but he's writing a brutal tragedy, full of suffering.

Oh, I have more faith in God than that. You're

not a man of faith, I can tell. I've read His wise words in the pages of Moses and Solomon and His words resound within me. And I know that His stories and my own story will all end up fine.

You're deluding yourself, friend. Explain for me how the Holocaust lines up with that positive story being written.

You're right, it is hard to fathom why bad things happen to innocent people. But bad things aren't all that happens; there's also goodness and love.

Yeah, that goodness and love sure helped everyone during the Holocaust and every other genocide in history.

You look upset, friend. Perhaps you've lost your love just like I did, and that's why you're upset. Perhaps it was the love of the only one who you desired. But it's going to be okay. You yourself told me that over the phone when you saved me. It's important for you to know that the pain you feel is real and valid.

I was too shocked by the idea that I needed him to validate my feelings that I couldn't tell him to shut up, so he kept fucking my brain with his words.

There's no pain greater than the pain you feel right now. Even if it was as small as a paper cut, that pain would be the worst you'd ever known in your whole life, because of all the deep cuts and weltering bruises and broken bones and shattered hopes and dreams that you've had, the paper cut is the only one you feel now and so it's the most severe and it's the worst. All the other pains have faded and are abstract. But this isn't a paper cut that you're suffering from. It's a seemingly unending gash oozing blood.

I'd recovered enough from his ridiculous comments to try and interject, but he kept barreling on.

I'm going to tell you something that you won't want to hear but that you need to hear. You are loved. Maybe you're not loved by the one who you want to love you. That's a tough truth to accept. But the comforting reality is that there are people out there who do love you. And guess what? You deserve that love! And eventually you'll find the love you want, and you'll receive it exactly as you want it and need it. It'll take some time. You might have to wait some chapters. But it's there for you if you'll be patient. I know you. You have the beautiful capacity to help people. That's so rare in this world. The fact that you cared about me enough to help me out when I was in such a bad place renewed my hope in life. We've all been put here to look out for and guide each other through this crazy world we live in. We can help each other make the best out of it. I aspire to help others the same way you helped me. You saved me, yes, you really did, and I'm sure that you save so many others each and every day. Maybe one day you'll save us all.

I headed inside, almost running away from that fucking Joseph, that crazed lunatic, fucking optimist, flaming romantic, group hugger, lover of life, lonely self-deluder, ancient shaman liar man. I flung the front doors open, propelling myself up those creaky, churning steps, shunning the bright joyous images on the windows. My coworkers tried drowning me in a wave of "you are loved"s, but I managed to scurry past them to my cubicle.

I sat in the peace of my Happiness Receptacle to start my mission. I had to send them all to hell. No. I had to send them back to the eternal purgatory they were already living in. It was my duty to open their eyes to the truth of the world they called home. Then they could exist in the world as they were meant to.

Joseph was right. It was my destiny to save them all. I buckled in to get to work and almost immediately got a call.

Hello. How may I save you today?

What?

Sorry, I mean, what's your problem? Why are you depressed?

Who said I was depressed?

Well, you called in, didn't you?

Yeah, but I'm not depressed. How dare you assume my mental state, you neuro-normative peasant.

Look, let's take a step back, I think we got off on the wrong foot. I want to help you. Can you please tell me where you are on the Sad-Happy Meter?

Definitely in the negatives.

Geez, that's not good. And what did you say your name was, ma'am?

Erin.

Hi Erin. My name's Jay. You know, my middle name's actually Aaron.

Wow, we have so much in common.

Look, you're clearly not doing too good on the Sad-Happy Meter. What's the matter?

Well, I haven't left my room in a few days. I'm stuck in this endless loop of thinking about the squirrels and the forests and how we're killing the planet.

Oh, well, why do you think we're killing the planet?

Think? How could you not know that we are? We've overpopulated the Earth!

We were getting callers like this lady more and more frequently. The more the earth seemed to degrade, and the more the media riled the people up with their doomsday predictions, the more frequently these bleeding-heart types kept being on the verge of exploding.

She continued: There's billions and billions and billions of us. We keep reproducing unsustainably. Meanwhile, the chickens are being slaughtered in cages so small they can't even stand up in them, and their eggs are gobbled up from inside their bodies, and Kentucky Fried Chicken sells the chicken's souls for so cheap, even though their employees are still severely underpaid because the minimum wage hasn't risen in decades, and we keep having more babies and throwing them into this mean and unfriendly world, even though there's still so many hungry people in Sierra Leone and Bangladesh and Uzbekistan. And now I'm pregnant because my boyfriend didn't want to use a condom because he said he didn't want anything to get in the way of our love and I can't get an abortion because there's mean people protesting shouting that I'm a killer outside of Planned Parenthood, and all I want to do is save the baby's life from a world it's too perfect for.

Wow. I'm sorry that the world is so awful. It seems like you want to spare your baby the pain of being brought into such a world.

I do. It deserves better.

Kinda makes you think, doesn't it?

About what?

About what you deserve.

Well, what do you mean?

I mean, if you want to save your child from having to suffer through such an awful life, then wouldn't you deserve to avoid such horrible suffering too?

Hmmm, yeah, I guess you're right. I never really thought about it that way. It truly is an awful world, isn't it? That actually makes a lot of sense, now that I think about it. I do deserve better. I'm no different than my baby. We're in this together. Thank you, Jay.

Oh, well, it's my pleasure.

You know, it's kind of funny that I'm coming to this realization from someone who's so nice and kind; I didn't believe that there was anyone like that anymore. Maybe we'll meet again in a better world.

Yes, I think we will. So long.

So long, Erin.

Click. Go and find that better world of yours.

Well, that was easy. It wasn't too hard convincing

a person to end her life when she was already
convinced that humans were a cancer.

I helped save a few more people, with varying
degrees of difficulty, and then it was time to prepare
for my visit to the lair.

The Blissful Bureaucrat's basement cave had an
open-door policy, but his intimidating niceness was
infamous, so not many people went to see him. I got
the ideas in order for my presentation.

I descended the Optimistic Escalator, rapped out
a hollow knock and entered the dark cavern. The walls
reverberated the eerie chants of an overly positive
parrot.

A happy man was seated behind a burgundy desk.
Mr. Joey Joy, the Chief Executive of Elation.

A pair of eyes returned from their hibernation. His
body remained shrouded in the dark, but his teeth
shone out, smiling unnervingly. A sweet scent
pervaded the cave. It seemed like a mixture of
blueberry muffins and cotton candy.

Mr. Joy sat unmoving. I waited for a sign of life.
Finally, it seemed he awoke.

He called out gladly: Why hellllooooooo there,
friend. You are loved. I'm **so** glad that you took me up
on my open-door policy. How may I be of assistance
to you today?

No, Your Blissfulness, **you** are loved. Sir, I've got
a proposal for you. I think I've got something big on
my hands. I'm sure you know how bad it is out there.
People are suffering so gravely. They need our help.

And I have just the idea to bring our Happiness to the masses.

I've got to say, I'm intrigued, my boy. Here at the Happy Hotline, we're willing to go quite far outside of the proverbial box to raise the Happy Bars of our Customer-Friends. Please Jay, do tell.

So, I told him. He had no reticence to any of my proposals. He bought it all. The retreat. The perfect day to bring forth all those lonely souls. The separate retreats for men and for women. The finding of the light they'd lost within themselves. Helping them build their personal sanctuaries. The peace they would find within these sanctuaries. And the joy they would find in inviting others into their newly crafted temples.

We'd make sure they'd nurture their peace so much, they'd spread it to the whole world.

CHAPTER EIGHT

I was talking to the depressed veteran when I had a vision of my own funeral. He was droning on and on about his war traumas and how he missed those glorious days. The guns, the boys, the beers, the long nights, the early morning runs, the rank smell of death. It all tied up into one fucked-up bow that strangled him, holding him back from continuing on with his life. So, he kept stooping down, trying to scoop at those out-of-reach grains of memory, reaching to parse between the wheat and the chaff of the past but always remaining an arms-length away from ever deciphering any of it. My heart was with him; I had also served.

But I'd heard the story told one too many times. All the stories coalesced into a dull, incessant nag. I waited for them to join me on our American shores of reason, to shed their blankets of pain and worry like I had, but I knew they never would.

That time had passed. They clung to those days like the only days of companionship that they were, all the while secluding themselves in their torment, never remembering that they could recreate that wartime camaraderie on domestic soils.

The veteran's voice provided a soothing backdrop to my daydream. I turned the speaker on and set the phone down on my desk.

My funeral is exactly as it's supposed to be. The exact-right amount of people attend. Dead souls waiting for the hope of an ascent peep out from under their stones to join in the festivities.

Everyone is there and they're all listless. There's no rabbi. There are no sacramental customs to commence. No one needs to scoop out dirt with an upturned shovel. Just an empty hole awaits my body. Everyone lingers, searching for someone to initiate the ceremonies.

Birds gather around the barren treetops, chirping greetings to each other. Deer dig through the snow to munch on grass as squirrels dart between those Bambi legs, digging through the dirt, seeking forgotten treasure chests of nuts. A black bear crawls out of its hibernation and rests on its paws at the edge of the tree-line.

Chava's there, leaning against a tree, wearing sandals.

The dead gather around, swapping stories they'd heard told countless times. I'm to be buried with my kinfolk, those souls I'd saved. They each stand solemnly above their graves, saluting me on my descent.

The sun's absent. Clouds merge with the gray, lifeless land, coalescing in an infinite hemisphere of nothingness.

People mill about. At first, they maintain a grave reverence. But then they slip into old habits. A divorced aunt who used to pinch my cheeks shivers in a short black dress. She sidles up to a professor drinking from a bottle of wine and showers him with her brilliant, once-heard musings of Freud.

A former schoolmate who became a journalist goes around asking folks for insights into my tortured life, but everyone speaks warm words of love, and he gets trapped between dueling narratives. No matter; the story will make the front page; people eat up stories about the perplexing human condition. A tortured soul makes for a good protagonist. Someone who helped others but couldn't help himself, they'd think. But I'd eventually helped myself like I'd helped all the rest.

Hannah's daughter perches on her mother's round shoulders, while Hannah babbles on to anyone who'll listen, trying to convince them of my deep conviction that life was worth living; I had merely tripped and fallen on the accidentally loaded shotgun.

All their strivings would come to nothing. They'd all join me in my temple soon enough. But their unwillingness to voluntarily enter the sanctuary entraps them in the mangled crevices of the temple walls, smelling the sweet air of the inner sanctum with one nostril while simultaneously being bludgeoned with the putrid stench of decay in the hairs of the other nostril.

Eventually, someone prods someone else to action. I sit upright in my throne as I'm led to my cherished, long-awaited home.

Eulogies are given. Someone talks about my courageous embrace of the world. How I went wherever I wanted to go, did whatever I wanted to do, lived without fear, sought counsel only in my own conscience. They tell the drunken-beaver dynamite story, how it all went wrong and yet exploded so beautifully right. The pond-hockey moose story. Whiskey sailing on the Mississippi, of course. All the good ones.

Someone speaks of destiny. Another person speaks of fate. Great orations filter out to the masses, regaling them with sanitized tales depicting the great meaning in life, all lies. But they're the lies the people want, and so they're content.

The people file out of the sacred grounds, words of praise gushing from their lips. They'll return to make pilgrimage. They must return to heed and remember my teachings.

I could come to them in dreams with visions of their tantalizing destinies, showing them the way. But why go to the trouble? I'd waited long enough to finally enjoy the peace and quiet of my new home. If they deserved the visions, they'd come seek me out.

Chava, after waiting for everyone else to leave, strides over to visit me. She takes the Star of David earrings I'd given her and lays them upon me. She looks back in my direction several times on her departure, regret stamped on her face.

Finally, I'm alone, free to move about as I wish. But I'm comfortable; there's no need to hurry off anywhere. I relax, waiting for all those pilgrims to come visit me.

I blinked my eyes and looked around my Happiness Receptacle. The veteran had continued talking all through my reverie.

Perhaps I shouldn't have daydreamed about my funeral. It wouldn't matter who would attend or how they'd send me off, since nothing mattered. Yet I was only human. I've put so much good into the world, I couldn't help but want a little appreciation for it.

I decided to stop José before I could slip into another fantasy, so I picked up the phone and cut him off.

Sorry, I missed that, José, what were you saying about the war? You know what, never mind. I'll tell you what, we're putting on a retreat in a couple of months, and I think you should come. It's all completely sponsored, all you gotta do is show up and we'll give you the help you need. That's great, José. I'll see you there. Remember, you are loved.

CHAPTER EIGHT

I was stopped by an urban farmer as he put up his deer fencing. Snow covered his rich soil. A greenhouse sheltered small crops of spinach and mustard greens. He'd have to wait nearly half a year before his next outdoor harvests.

The wind beat against the thin plastic of the greenhouse. Leaning against his half-built fence, he waved me over.

Can you give me a hand here for a second?

Sure, sir. How's it going? Must suck working outside in the winter. I'm sure you'd rather be somewhere in the Caribbean plucking bananas in the sun and surfing during your lunch break.

You know what? I actually enjoy the winters here. They're brutal, no doubt, but it's good having the off-season. Lets you focus on other things. Don't have to have your hands in the dirt 24/7. My heart actually goes out to those tropical farmers. The fruits there are always popping like crazy. Things that are annual here are perennial there. The tomatoes always grow, peppers, you name it. It's a blessing, sure, to live with that abundance, but it's also a curse. You're always in the same routine. It's easier, but not necessarily better. You go through the same routine over and over again. You never get to can your veggies in the fall. There's no pickling. No jams. No salsa. Sure, you can do all those things, but you don't really need to. Everything's always fresh. I like the variance of the seasons here.

We lifted the fence together and dropped it into the holes he'd dug for it. I closed my jacket tighter around me.

Damn, what are you, a Thomas Jefferson philosopher farmer? Just admit you fucking hate this cold.

Can't do it, my friend. I wouldn't get to sharpen my tools in front of the fireplace while I listen to Prince records if not for the cold. Wouldn't get to plot out my fields for the next season, coordinating that beautiful symphony of abundance, imagining all those neatly lined rows that never turn out as they look on paper but are still perfect in their own way just the same. Wouldn't get to lift my face up to the sun in the summer and truly drink in its warmth because I remember all these frigid winter days where my fingers grow numb with the work. That doesn't mean I don't love these days, too. They're great, in their own way. It's a beautiful life, man.

If you keep telling yourself that, one day you might actually believe yourself.

If you're so cynical, feel free to come out and work with me for a day. I think everyone should get their hands dirty once in a while. Get back to working with the Earth. I don't have anything for you to do this time of year, but you should come back through in the springtime if you're interested.

I don't think I'm going to take you up on that one, sir, but you enjoy.

I bustled down those cold, lonesome streets, leaving the farmer to his joyful labors. I stepped into a combo gas station and mechanic shop for a pack of smokes. A greasy mechanic chatted happily with the clerk. He stopped and turned in my direction.

Say, what's a big guy like you do with all those muscles?

I blushed. Who, me?

You see anyone else in here with softballs for biceps?

It must be the jacket, man. You're seeing things.

Nah, you look like a sturdy fella. Look like you know how to use tools. We're actually looking to bring someone on. It's a great job. Get to tinker around with some fun cars. We had a '72 Mercedes SE in here the other day. It's a fun one. Why don't you come join us?

Jesus, everyone's trying to get me to work for them today. I'm gainfully employed, thank you very much.

Ah, but being employed and enjoying what you're doing are two vastly different things my friend.

Man, everyone's a fucking armchair psychologist in this town.

He tucked his hands into his front jacket pockets and smiled at me.

Them's your words, buddy, not mine. But I'm sure whatever work you're doing wearing those fancy pants and shoes won't fit you near as good as wearing some worn jeans and boots, with some grease under your nails. There's nothing like letting the hot water run the dirt offaya at the end of an honest day's work, having a nice dinner with your wife, going to bed contented and falling asleep with no worries. I been reading about your generation and all your sleep problems. All these gadgets you all got now just to fall asleep. Bogus babbling brooks blaring out over blasted speakers just so you can remember what being tired's like. I hear they started putting little kids on sleeping pills now too. It's disgraceful. Parents gotta let the kids run around in circles outside and they'll tire themselves out. But they keep feeding them their tofu and kale and whatnot and putting them in therapy and then they wonder why they're so screwed up. Got 'em thinking too much and not doing nothing. You look too smart and strong to fall into that trap. Come join us in the garage for a day. You'll have the time of your life.

Thank you, sir, but I sleep like a baby at night.

Ah, but you don't find your meaning during the day.

And who are you to say that? I know exactly why I'm doing my job. My job is my meaning. In fact, I get paid to help other people find their meaning.

Oh, and what's their meaning?

Well … let's just say I help them face their fears and overcome the lives the world tells them they have to lead.

Well, sounds like we agree on that at least. There's a severe culture shift you young folks need, mark my words on that. Well, if you ever change your mind, there's always more cars need fixin.

He wiped his forehead with the back of his hand, leaving a trail of black oil. Nodding to me, he turned back to chat with his pal over the counter. I left without buying anything and threw the door open, leaving the psychologists to their tools of reason.

I crossed the bridge over the frozen river and walked over to the college side of town. Children ran through the cold playing hide and seek. A serene man stood by his lonesome in the bludgeoning cold holding a sign: LIFE ISN'T THE HOAX EITHER. DYNASTIES DIE. NEITHER THE ICE NOR THE WATER.

I threw him a quizzical look. He only pointed to his brain. It was all obvious. Cryptic messages held up on street corners logical only to the writer, trying to change the masses' minds; don't get soaked up in the people's long-standing, never-considered beliefs, pursue your truth. Tell yourself you're making an impact by putting the truth out there. You've got the right idea, man. It was all so clear.

I kept walking along the river. They were holding a book-reading at Red Georgie's. I stepped inside just as the book reading was wrapping up. Red Georgie thanked the author for her insights. The crowd clapped. Books were signed at the back of the room.

Eager youths couldn't wait to get home and read her truths. I intercepted some at the front. They'd do fine at the retreat. Come join the crowd of people just like you. Think, walk and act like you. Live like you. Suffer like you.

A pair of freshmen babbled excitedly. One taut and rigid and intense, the other calm, relaxed and loose.

The intense one was talking. Oh, it's the idea of the century for sure. You're on to it, Abe. All we gotta do is figure out how to build it.

What's the great concept, boys?

They turned red with the inevitable blush that accompanies being so sure of a great insight, yet still so young.

Oh, I was just telling Kane about this app idea I had. I can't tell you the exact specifics, obviously, but, well, I guess I'll put it like this: What if you could know what your past life was like? Exactly what happened, who you were, where you lived, all your successes and failures, everything that tripped you up, the lucky things that helped you on your way. It connects your soul to a past soul, one exhibiting your exact-same personality and characteristics, biases, proclivities, perversions, whatever. Every day that passes in our lives does not return. So, you can see how you acted wrong in a past life and figure out whatever corrections you need to make. Then, you could live your life as if for a second time, with all the wisdom of the previous time. It would be like taking your developed mind now and putting it into a baby and going through everything that happened in your life again. Think about how many buckets you'd get playing basketball with a sharp mind against little middle schoolers sprouting pimples for the first time. All the tests you'd ace, the girls you'd seduce. It would be almost too easy. You could do everything exactly like you always wanted to. But maybe I've said too much. Can we trust you?

You're safe with me, boys. I might be a time traveler come back from your future life to encourage you. I'm impressed; you've found something new under the sun. The two of you should come through to the Hotline retreat I'm putting on. You can put your app to the test with the people there. It's going to be on Valentine's Day at Lake Minnetonka. Come to think of it, why don't I join you all in your app venture? I have the backing of the Hotline, so we can make it really big. I have an idea, too. What if, instead of a single past life, we programmed for all past lives?

Yeah, we might be able to do that.

I think we could.

Great. Why don't you guys give me your numbers and we'll meet up and plan this thing out. I'll be in touch.

Sure thing. That sounds great! Can't wait to hear from you.

The other one agreed: Yeah, for sure, that would be great, sir. We could get the app into the hands of every man and woman in America if the Hotline was behind it!

The boys hurried out with the rest of the

dispersing crowd. I'd found the kids; they'd be a great help. But I didn't recruit hardly anyone to the retreat. The masses still needed to drink my elixir, but there were only so many people you could recruit at the subversive bookstores. Door-to-door salesmanship would take too long. But there were other ways to advertise the retreat. I just had to set the cameras up and get the stage ready. Then they'd come. And we'd be able to save them.

Every day that passes does not return. Gotta give it to the kid; that's a good insight. Every day that passes does not return. Thank the fucking Lord.

CHAPTER EIGHT

The boys were eager to be on set and see the commercial's production.

So Jay, who's directing it?

We got the Coen brothers.

The two kids started babbling to each other.

No shit. I like them. That one religious movie of theirs was pretty bullshit though. Made no sense.

Oh, I liked that one.

I thought it was okay.

Nah, it fucking sucked. The dude though. Now that's a fucking classic.

I'm all about those white Russians.

We should go and do some bowling later.

Not a bad day for it. Be nice to stay indoors with this weather.

You know I'm always down for a good bowl.

Their rambling was getting annoying. Listen, I'll take you guys once the shoot's wrapped up for the day. We can work on the app over some beers. Here, come take a look at what we've got so far for the commercial. It's pretty much all done. We just have to film and incorporate one final shot of Adam and Eve naked in the garden planting a seed in the ravaged dirt as a meteorite looms on the horizon. And then it'll fade into the outro and tagline: Find Your Meaning — The Happy Hotline Retreat. The screen's over here; check it out.

The black screen turns into cascading waterfalls in a lush forest.

A man types on his laptop in a solar-paneled treehouse. He shoots off an email. A white-robed man pops up on the screen, and every screen throughout the world, reading a divine proclamation from a scroll.

"Man has reached his limits. The balance must be restored. Everything I created for you will remain. Everything your vanity has driven you to create will be purged. You will be naked with Me once more, as you have not been since you ate My forbidden fruits. I will restore all your creations on one condition: You must succeed in recreating the '65 Mustang. It was My personal favorite of all your inventions. Oh, and make it cherry-red."

A boom resounds in the sky. People topple down from vanishing airplanes, their naked bodies gently cascading as angels with feathery wings guide them into soft meadows just transformed back from asphalt runways. Silence and serenity. Lovers hold each other under apple trees. Streams flow down mountains, arriving past undammed waterways, dumping glassy-clear liquid into calm seas. Children play and skip in the sand. Old ladies wipe their asses with twigs and fallen leaves.

Manhattan Island. Millions of naked bodies frantically run in circles yelling for help and looking everywhere for food. They dive into the Hudson River, trying to reach the other side, where there might be enough resources to provide for everyone. Most of them drown on the way.

Tucson. The sun's still up, beating down on pale vulnerable flesh. They, too, run in circles, screaming for help, and they jump into the inviting arms of cacti, biting into its spiky flesh, pulp oozing down stabbed and gored faces.

Portland. Farmers harvest any available fruit from their vines, ripe or unripe. The farmers grab their children's hands and run up hillsides to wait it all out, but conniving brutes overrun them, tearing them limb from limb, devouring the thin child bodies raw along with the fields' tomatoes and cucumbers. Wolves, hyenas, lions, jaguars and dogs play the same yummy game with fat, slow humans who trudge along bloodily, collapsing in the dust, waiting to be devoured.

The sun goes up, the sun goes down, the sun goes up, the sun goes down, the moon flits in and out, the sun goes up, big step back, zoom out.

Numbers scrawl on the screen. Population one-tenth of what it once was. Scratch the numbers out. Make that one-twentieth.

Sun goes up, sun goes down, sun goes up, sun goes down, moon goes up. Mosquitoes menace the people. Starving families scratch oozing itches. Sweaty, feverish babies are left in the dust of windswept plains. Hive-ridden bodies are left behind boulders. People dream about warm, sealed homes, homes with air conditioning, showers and stoves.

Sun goes up, snow falls down. Old bearded men go out for one final hug of the Earth's floor. The snow blankets and encrusts their long beards. Numbers on the screen. 11 million left, but then the numbers fade.

Sun goes down, moon goes up, moon goes down, sun goes up, bees buzz, birds chirp, chipmunks scurry, bears emerge, chickens go bok bok bokee. Primitive clothes are fashioned out of fig leaves. Small bands of brothers and sisters and cousins and acquaintances and dirty, dusty, persevering survivors make their way north along the rivers. Eagles soar. Crafty, rough canoes are burned out of lightning-struck oaks and chestnuts and maples.

The sun goes up, the sun goes down, the sun goes up. Sketches are drawn up in the sand; a figure emerges of that glorious red Mustang that must be rebuilt. The dream churns on. Combustion engines appear in kaleidoscopic dreams. Metal rims revolve around and around, bearing black tires, etched into the trunks of trees.

Crude shovels dig for ore. A sail made out of tanned and stretched cowhide bears small boats down the Mississippi into the Gulf then east through the Caribbean, where fish are speared with wooden stakes, open seas are braved by men navigating using half-remembered constellations until the African shore is found and the Congo is sailed up, until rubber trees are found, where sign language is tossed about in the damp African air, where realization dawns of impressive progress as a group leads another to a set of four magnificent rubber tires and a steering wheel; praises are given and antelopes are roasted over a fire, as women dance and men chant over methodical drumbeats, while the past is reached back into, reached back, reached back, into the cloudy past reached back, and then whoosh fly forward into the blind future, head back down the Congo, cross the seas, head west through the islands up into the Gulf, up the Mississippi, and find the thriving clan in their orchards with the frame of the car all done, the engine miraculously seemingly ready, so put it all together, sacrifice lambs, also slit beautiful child heads that tumble pouring blood over the finished vehicle that's a red '65 Mustang, all done, so time to turn the finely-crafted metal key, but nothing happens, so spend days giving it a go this way and that, turn it over and over, maybe the corn oil won't work as gasoline even though Kenny's sketches made it all seem right, but it doesn't work, so keep the farms going, meanwhile the hunting and the clothes progress and nice merino wool sweaters are shipped upon bigger boats sailing across farther seas as populations increase and miners mine for oil, striking black gold and bringing it back home to try it out, but the Mustang doesn't start, so people fall down on their knees and cry, but the tears dry as they lie down prone in the sun. They bake there indifferently.

A new wave of smallpox goes around and mucky blisters pop up on bent-over vomiting bodies with no hope of a cure, devastating clans, and the sun goes up, the sun goes down. Lonely people struggle to light a fire in the rain, while deer and bison run through virgin fields with almost no one left in what's a fresh start the world over, but humans don't like beginning anew, so words flash through screens telling the masses what they must do, the world will die if we keep going down the same path as we have been, no, something must be done, the retreat, come join us, the car won't get built, or maybe we'll build it but it'll never run like before, so Find Your Meaning — The Happy Hotline Retreat.

I clicked off the screen. At the end, we have to put in Adam and Eve planting a fruit tree. Gotta end on a hopeful note or the networks will never run it. The brothers did a good job; it's right up their alley. They're no good when they try and extend themselves to other strains of philosophy and storytelling, but give them some absurd chaos and they do a good job.

One of the kids looked around the set and was confused: Those are the people you got to play Adam and Eve? They're built for Hollywood, not surviving the apocalypse. Those big muscles won't help them in the jungle. You gotta be smart and crafty. You know who's going to be the one to survive? A thin short couple who don't need to eat much to live and who've figured out how to build a fire and run for long periods to hunt the deer and bison across the prairie. Mr. Hollywood's gotta eat Michael Phelps levels of food. He'd starve in an afternoon.

True, but the people don't want to see that. They want to see a naked chiseled chest over iron thighs and piston calves. Gotta give them what they want. Well, that's the tour. I don't have time to go bowling now. I gotta make sure this final shot is done exactly right, but here's what I want you guys to do: Each of you make the app on your own. Then, we'll sit together and take the best aspects of each and make the perfect app for the people from the composite. We'll give the people those past lives they long for so badly.

CHAPTER EIGHT

I could see eagerness in the boys' faces and knew that we had a success.

So, boys, you've got the goods?

Yessir.

Great! Alright, Kane, you can offer yours up first.

Okay, so I veered off from the original idea a little bit, but I think that this app will be even bigger and better than the past-lives one. Here's the pitch: Have you ever wondered how you rank against your fellow humans in any specific category? This app lets you do that. So far, I've hacked into Facebook and Instagram and Google and Twitter and have created pretty concise rankings for about half of everyone who's alive right now, about 3.62 billion people, and I'm working on figuring out how to add in the rankings of everyone else alive. If I can figure that out, you'll be able to tell how you rank against over 7 billion people. The sky's the limit; you can determine pretty much any ranking you can imagine.

Abe piped up: That's so amazing, bro! I know the one ranking that I'd never ever want to know. I'd never fucking want to know how I rank against other people for how much time I've spent jacking off. No way in hell. I'd probably be top ten in the world. Fuck that, I'm happy not knowing that one.

Haha, for sure. But think about all the things you could know. You could figure out what number runner you are in the whole world, or how good of a basketball player you are, or guitar player, or how good you are at math. That's a good one; imagine if you place five billionth in that, then, you know, that's something you gotta work on and if you get good at it you could crack the top billion or even top hundred million. We could finally prove once and for all that LeBron James is the greatest of all time and never have to convince all those haters. What about how good you are at breathing or sleeping or even thinking? It would add so much healthy competition to the world if everyone knew exactly how they and their friends ranked in all these things. You could make running clubs or art clubs or baking clubs where people get together and collaborate on improving and you'd get these elite teams that could get sponsorships from meditation apps and sleeping apps and all those things. And think about how easy it would be for businesses. If you could advertise that you're the literal No. 1 plumber in the entire country and rank 4th in the entire world, fuck, you'd be swimming in business. Hiring would be so easy. You simply find the young guys who are already really high in the rankings for their age and bring them on and teach them, and you'll get a behemoth of a firm, causing business to skyrocket. And artists and writers could finally know how they compare with their contemporaries. George Saunders would easily be the top living writer, and it would actually be pretty easy to rank him against former writers. You could just plug in their works. Shit, I could do that today. You plug in all the things they've written, and then you know that Saunders is the 91st best writer of all time and Steinbeck is the 5th best writer and Moses comes in as the best ever and Dostoevsky shockingly comes in at 15,347, way lower than you'd expect. Vonnegut would be high up, but Saul Bellow would be so low because he fucking blows. And it works for everything. Think about how much we could charge for subscriptions. Think about all those Top 100 lists that *Rolling Stone* puts out all the time. We could prove how fucking wrong they were with all their bullshit rankings. The only thing they ever got right was that Jimi was the number one guitarist, but Bob Dylan as the 7th best singer of ever? Are you fucking kidding me? He's the 4,661,820,693rd best singer in the world. Doesn't even crack the top half of singers all time. We could charge 50 bucks a pop for people to have access to these rankings of the best artists of all time, and 100 or 200 or fuck, even a grand for the personal rankings. Who's gonna say no to getting to know their ranking? You could know exactly how you rate against everyone else.

For sure bro, that's amazing. I'd love to know how I rank among app developers. I'd probably be fucking Top 100. You know how fucking sick that is? And everyone else can see that, too? You know how easy that would make it to get laid? You don't even have to use a pickup line at a bar, since girls will see your ranking and come up to you, throwing their legs spread wide open, asking you to take them so they can say they got to bang one of the top developers in human history. It would be fucking amazing.

Yeah, bro, and that's not even the best part. Think about all of the government and military applications. If you sold those rankings with exclusive rights to the United States government, I mean, shit. How much could you sell that for? 10 billion? 50? So that they could know how good every soldier and officer and general is, and could also know how to wage every battle or whether a battle isn't worth fighting in the first place, since the enemy has the greatest living general ready to face off against you? Fuck bro. The opportunities are endless.

And you didn't even mention universities. It would make hiring professors and deciding what students to admit so easy. Fuck affirmative action and determining admissions based on race or gender or class or whatever the fuck arbitrary, infantile human rankings we've had for how many millennia; we'd make all that completely anachronistic, and it would be so easy to call any institution out on their bullshit because there would be complete transparency. Oh, so there's a rich kid who ranks in the bottom 3 percent of all students in America, but you accepted him into Stanford on a rowing scholarship, even though the boy's never picked up an oar in his life? My fucking ass the public would be okay with that. Damn, bro. You're a fucking genius.

Thanks, bro.

Anytime, bro.

I couldn't take it anymore: Are you fucking me right now?

What?

I said are you fucking me right now?

Um, do you mean am I fucking you by helping you create the app of the century and making you billions of dollars?

I'll get back to you in a minute, Kane — I turned to Abe — I sure hope that you have something good for me. Like we planned.

Um, yeah, yeah, I did the app we talked about, I got it up and running. Here, you can check all your past lives. Look into the camera and put your thumb on the home button.

No, it's not for me. You do it.

Okay.

Beep beep. Boop boop.

Past lives: First life: born 37th century BCE. Hevel son of Ish. Northern Israel. Lived until 36th century BCE. Death by betrayal. Worst moment: Getting into a fight with his brother the farmer. Best moment: Shepherding his flock in the foothills of the Golan Heights as the clouds rolled in over the Sea of Galilee. (Click here to see more on Hevel)

Second life: born 36th century BCE. Boulder BO36ME11LB. Southern coast of Lebanon. Lived 200 yards from shore, 50 feet from stream, 5 feet from palm tree PT03ME11LB. Lived until 11th century CE. Died by gradual erosion. Worst moment: One time in the 4th century CE a young boy accidentally stepped on the jagged edge of Boulder BO36ME11LB and gashed his foot, leading to an infection and eventual death. Best moment: Watching two people in the 9th century CE make passionate love at sunset under palm tree PT08ME10LB, three feet from Boulder BO36ME11LB's astonished and thrilled gaze. (Click here to see more on Boulder)

Third Life: born 11th century CE. Loggerhead Sea Turtle LT11ME14MT. Mediterranean Sea wanderer. Lived until 14th century CE. Death by heartbreak. Worst moment: when Loggerhead Sea Turtle LT13ME15MT abandoned him for Loggerhead Sea Turtle LT12ME15MT. Best moment: when Loggerhead Sea Turtle LT13ME15MT told him she'd be with him forever and ever and ever. (Click here to see more on Turtle)

Fourth Life: born 14th century CE. Deer DE14EU14GR. Peloponnesian Peninsula. Lived until 14th century CE. Death during birth. Worst moment: Leaving Deer DE13EU14GR's womb. Best moment: Leaving Deer DE13EU14GR's womb. (Click here to see more on Deer)

Fifth Life: born 14th century CE. Pine Tree PT14EU17GR. Peloponnesian Peninsula. Lived until 17th century CE. Death by axe. Worst moment: Being axed. Best moment: When best friend Pine Tree

PT15EU18GR grew up 10 feet away and their roots touched underground 15 years later. (Click here to see more on Tree)

Previous Life: built 17th century CE. Ottoman Trading Vessel TV17EU20TU. Lived until 20th century CE. Death by Seattle museum fire. Worst moment: When the flames finally leapt up onto the deck of the ship, burning boat down excruciatingly board by board. Best moment: When Captain Cezayirli Gazi Hasan Pasha sailed into Istanbul for the first time in the 18th century as the sun set over the harbor. (Click here to see more on Vessel)

I felt a powerful burst of happiness emanating within me, graciously accepting his work.

Perfect, that's exactly what we need. Great job, Abe. I couldn't be happier. This will do the job for sure. We'll launch it at the retreat; it'll work perfectly. As for you, Kane. You might as well fucking delete that shitty app you made and get on board with the program. Abe's got a great app going. Look, you're talented. I'm sure you could help Abe out with his app and make it even better.

Kane was seething and looked like he wanted to hurt someone. Why are you angry? You didn't do what I told you to do. That doesn't mean you can't still help us. Look, we don't need a stupid program to tell us that Abe's app is the best app ranked against all the other apps. We'll know it's the best because it'll work. And it'll change the world forever.

CHAPTER EIGHT

Where is Abe?

I don't know.

Are you sure that's the answer you want to go with?

I said I don't know.

What did you do?

I only did what you sent me out to do.

What I sent you out to do? No. Clearly, you didn't understand the problem I had with your app. I didn't accept Abe's work instead of yours because I favored him over you. Your app was forgone because it lies to people. It tells them that there's some kind of meaning in their lives. It assumes that everyone on the rankings is important and that you're important because you're first or that you're important because you're last. Whoever you are, you can strive for something. You can work hard and improve and rise up the ranks. Or you can tank and be proud that you're the lamest and laziest fucker on Earth. There are even some people who'll strive to get to the exact middle of all humanity; they'll seek to be the perfectly average Joe, indomitable and awesome in their mediocrity. You clearly don't understand humans. You used your fertile fields of insight to try to feed them lies. Abe's app does the opposite. It leads them on a path to enlightenment. It sends them on a spiral of discovery where they can sift through all of their other unmeaningful past lives. Then, they'll finally understand that neither those lives nor this life ever amounted to anything. They could live another fifty lives and they would still never amount to anything meaningful. I accepted his app because he did as I asked and gave himself up to my vision entirely. You didn't do that. You had to pursue your own idea even when I expressly told you to work on something else.

I thought you'd like it.

But you didn't kill him because you were disappointed, you killed him out of jealousy.

How do you know what I did?

Well, where's Abe if you didn't kill him?

Um…

Look, you don't have to worry about me reporting you. I understand what happened. You didn't mean to kill him. You got into a fight. It got out of hand. Maybe you bashed his head into the pavement, and maybe it felt good to do it. And maybe you did it one more time than you meant to.

That's right! I didn't want him to die.

But he did. And now you will be cursed for it. Almost in a biblical manner. Your app will succeed just as you wanted it to, but you'll gain no pleasure from its success. You'll make more money than you could ever know what to do with, but you'll feel cold and empty forever. Your money will provide no comfort to you, blankets won't warm you, nor will the tender warmth of a woman.

But I thought that what you wanted out of the app was to prove that nothing mattered, so why does what I did to Abe matter?

Murder isn't the way, you fool. It defeats the whole purpose. Murder sends the deceased up to heaven a martyr. No matter what sins he committed, he'll slip his way past the pearly gates. Murder takes the fun out of the game. It forces the victim to embrace God and the world and the soul of the universe when he never wanted to and never would've if he'd had the choice. You're right that nothing matters. But the fact that nothing matters only matters if the people can realize it and self-actualize it. You robbed Abe of that opportunity. If he'd chosen his own death, he could've had an eternity of nothing mattering and would've reaped the beautiful rewards for that understanding.

Kane shook his head, not comprehending, so I explained further. You see, there's a special bliss you get when you cast off the heavy burden of caring. You feel it the second the knife plunges through your temporary distraction of a conscience, releasing you into the wonderful intermediary world of believing in non-belief, which you can bask in forever. What is this world? It's the island. It's forever waiting on the tepid shores, looking out into an opaque haze of a 55-degree day with a sprinkle of rain coming down. There's never a clear sky, nor a full-on downpour, just that light, ever-present mist. The water seeps into your clothes, keeping you in an interminable state of ultra-consciousness. Your hairs stand forever on end, your body's finger forever hovering over the switch of your fight or flight mode, but never flipping it up or down. It's a beautiful place. A paradise. You, Kane, will never enter this place. You'll linger in this worthless world on the cusp of that world, hearing the light lapping of waves on the shores of the island, but you'll never find it, nor will you remember that you're supposed to seek it out.

So, what do I do?

First, you retrieve Abe's app and bring it to me. Then, you put out your app and reap the harvest of your labors. Then, you wander the world, forever searching for a meaning that you will never find. Oh, and don't you dare think of deleting his app and escaping me. There are far worse punishments that I could give you. But this is the appropriate one.

But I'll go out into society and they'll see my success and be jealous of me and kill me. I guess I don't really mind that, it's as good as suicide to me.

No, they won't kill you. That release will forever elude you as well, the one you forced on your friend. The people will feel the coldness on you and flee from you. They'll feel nothing toward you, neither intense love nor fear nor anger. You'll find a woman and she'll bear your seed, but she'll only be with you for your wealth. She'll neither love nor pity you; you'll be nothing to her other than the father of her children and the signer of her checks. You'll see her raise your children and you'll see your children have children and their children have children, but they'll be like strangers to you. You'll start heading east and then continue circling the globe around and around, never finding peace. Now, go and face your destiny.

CHAPTER EIGHT

After securing the app and getting it up and running, I headed back into the dim light of the cave. Teeth glimmered toward me through the dark.

Helllloooooo there, friend. You are loved. So, how's the retreat coming along? You got everything ready?

Yeah, we're getting there, the team's doing some fine work.

And?

And? Oh, you are loved, sir, you are loved.

And you, too, are loved. Please, call me Mr. Joy.

Of course, Mr. Joy.

So, the team's doing good work?

Oh, yes sir, Mr. Joy.

Good. The team's the most important thing. If there's one thing I've learned in my many years helping people, it's that it's all about the people you surround yourself with. Surround yourself with some good people and they'll make everything so smooth you'll feel like you're coasting on the fair breezes of the Mediterranean, even if you're caught in these damned Minnesota blizzards. You know, I went out on a limb giving you this huge project, but something I saw in your eyes convinced me to trust you. I saw how much you want to help people. It's your driving mission.

That's true, sir. I do want to help people, more than anything.

Mr. Joy looked me up and down and then grabbed my shoulder.

Say, let's get outta here. I love this cave but sometimes I gotta get out into the world. Let's go play some golf.

Golf, Mr. Joy? How are we going to play golf with all the snow on the ground?

Oh, don't worry son. I got a spot.

The mansion stood monstrous beside the A-frame houses dotting the lake's edge. An iron gate opened to a long driveway. The house's immaculate stone-masoned exterior was full of fireplaces and Roman arches. These wove in seamlessly with the timber-framed terrace and hand-hewn log wall siding.

Animals of all types resided in the yard. Bald eagles looked out from behind enormous golden cages in the low branches of oak trees. Wolves strode back and forth in their enclosure, which adjoined that of a family of deer. Bears snored deeply in their hibernation behind plexiglass.

We headed inside to golf as only the richest of the rich can, on a private indoor country club eighteen. The clubs and balls were real, but when you struck the ball it would shoot off into a nearby net. This net would absorb the ball and shoot off an exact virtual replica down the fairway with the same trajectory, spin and velocity as the real one. The new virtual ball might then careen down corridors, bounce off windows, or, if you were skillful like Mr. Joy, end up very close to the hole, where a real ball would pop up from the floor, allowing you to putt it home.

The course wove through the mansion, up and down seven floors, past the movie theatre, through the bowling alley, by the suspended shark tank, in between the racquetball gym and the basketball court and over the Olympic sized pool and the hot tubs designed in the shape of the solar system.

In between meticulously studied shots, Mr. Joy introduced me to his cherished friends. When the Hotline was doing so well that Mr. Joy and his potential progeny would never again have to worry about living expenses, Mr. Joy moved all his friends to the mansion. They were ecstatic to get to relive their fraternity glory days. They spent their time playing basketball, drinking kegs of beer, discoursing on philosophical treatises and east Asian geopolitics and, of course, chasing tail.

The group, nicknamed the Jubilant Joyfriends, spent those first days in pure bliss, going on hunting trips, drinking beers by the fire, having the chefs cook them up meal after meal of foie gras and eel and bison steaks and anything else they could imagine; they could've had their asses wiped for them if they wanted. Eventually, however, the bowling and duck hunting and ice skating on the backyard rink got stale and the

Jubilant Joyfriends got restless.

Mr. Joy would return from work to great orgies of bourbon waterfalls and chocolate fountains and, of course, real man-woman orgies, but the squad got bored; there were only so many times you could skewer a rabbit over the grill and wash it down with home-brewed wheat beers before you looked for something else to do. A restlessness overcame the group and they thought about incorporating more interesting prey into their hunting expeditions, but that was too cliché for bored rich people. Besides, this was a philosophical and considerate group.

So, their restlessness turned on the one working member of the squad, Mr. Joy, who had enough of their complaining and whining. He finally solved his problem by bringing them all into the Hotline as branch leaders.

Mr. Joy assigned all of his friends jobs according to their skills and temperaments.

Zach was a marine biologist, so he got the lead gig on the Dolphins for the Depressed branch, where he oversaw a team of 135 people who combatted the sadness of the town's common folk, who were caught up in the everyday struggle of working too hard for too little pay, and who had far too few dolphins in their lives.

Jack came in to grow medicinal marijuana to help recover people's lost appetites as they went through chemo.

Dan led the Yurts for Vets campaign that brought

veterans together in farming communities, where they could raise livestock for slaughter, putting their bloodlust to good use.

Chandler was on top of the Tits for Tots drive that connected moms who'd lost their newborns to working moms who couldn't be with their babies to feed them all day. Chandler was very passionate about tits.

Russell led the political science division. He'd worked for boutique polling companies in his post-grad days and harbored great dreams like those of all his former classmates of one day imposing his vision on the shoulders of a great and charismatic man. Mr. Joy placed him in charge of the newly formed Vote branch of the Hotline, there to encourage all the citizens of the country that their little solitary votes did indeed matter. It was on each of us to use our privilege of living in a 21st century democracy to pay tribute to all those lost souls who'd starved in the gulags of the millennia, wishing for a chance to vote out their inebriated, corrupt, hereditary-lottery-winning leaders.

While spreading the power of the individual vote was the branch's main goal, the bulk of Russell's time in the office was spent designing the candidacy and campaign of His Greatness LeBron James.

He was deemed the perfect man to lead the country. It was all so simple. LeBron did it for the children. He was all about education. He'd win you all the mom votes, 100 percent. Russell would have him run as an independent, because LeBron was above the bullshit politicking of the major parties, but he'd have highly liberal platforms, so he'd win California in a landslide, and that's before even accounting for the championships he'd win now that he'd moved to LA.

He'd automatically win the Ohio and Florida votes from the time he put in there. Massachusetts would be a tough sell, those fucking Celtics fans don't give up a grudge, but the office could be won without them. The way Russell saw it, it was pretty much a cinch. Get him a good Vice President like Mark Cuban, who'd bring in all the economically minded Republicans and Texas? Oh, it was a done deal, you could've put him in the Oval Office last week.

The sky was the limit. Russell had crunched the numbers for years. The path was all set. Give LeBron six more years to rack up some more championships and play a little with his son Bronny, one term as the mayor of Akron, one term as governor of Ohio and the presidency was his in 2032. And the first day in office LeBron would condense the states from 50 to 22 hyper-efficient regional centers of commerce. The country would experience the greatest economic boom in its history.

Of course that'll work, Russell. Good to know all those tax-free donations are being spent so well to ensure the betterment of the country, nay, the world.

All of the friends were experts and, with Mr. Joy's financing, were able to ply their trades in an altruistic fashion instead of selling out and slaving for the new-age aristocracy.

Mr. Joy led me by the arm. I still haven't given you the complete master tour. We have to check out the tunnels.

The tunnels?

Of course we have tunnels. You think we'd walk out to the party barn in three feet of snow?

The tunnels stretched endlessly underground, wide enough to fit a military jeep, from the basement of the house to the guest house to underneath the party barn. The barn served as a venue for decadent community gatherings, and for an annual black-tie fundraising dinner. Mr. Joy also let the local cops use it for their holiday parties, as well as letting them use the pools and basketball court and gym, to ensure he stayed in their good graces.

Well, whaddaya think?

What could I think, sir? It's incredible. This place must have cost a pretty penny.

Oh, it was nothing. Definitely worth the investment. You don't know how many strings you can pull when you got a place like this to offer the cops and the city council. So, kid, you getting excited for the retreat?

You know what? I am. But I also miss the thrill of getting to help people out on a day-to-day basis. The last few weeks have all been budgets and logistics and planning. Don't get me wrong, it's a great opportunity, but there's something about getting to hear someone's voice over the phone as you're helping them.

Son, I'll tell you what: I was exactly like you when

I was younger. Thinking that for each person who I helped find their lost light and joy, it was as if I was saving a world. But if I've learned one thing over my years helping people, it's that investing in philanthropy at a larger scale pays off. Helping people one by one is nice. It's cute, it makes you feel something, but doing it on a grand stage is where you'll effect real change.

Really?

Sure. Think about how many people there are in the world. You think that holding people's hands and helping them one at a time is anything more than a drop in the bucket? It's all about the raw numbers on the page. There are so many suffering souls out there. It's tempting to want to get to know each one of them. It feels better when you help them that way; it makes you feel important knowing that little Billy will grow up with a father who's there for him instead of a crack addict. But you're still only saving one person. When you save the masses, you don't get those personal stories, but you'll be putting more good into the world than you could imagine. It's all about the people, Jay.

He slapped me on the back.

You're gonna put on a hell of a retreat. You got any problems or need any help, you come to me. Good luck, son.

He walked me to the front gate, where his limo driver was waiting. I looked back at the animals in their enclosures and saw the lions pawing at the snow in their cages, munching on slabs of steak.

CHAPTER EIGHT

The lobby resounded with the echoes of nervous chatter. Scarves were unwrapped, gloves were shoved into coat pockets and coats were placed onto hangers. When the hangers ran out, the coats collected on the floor in a dizzying heap.

The storm was yet hundreds of miles to the west. There was still time to get on board and avoid the calamity. I still had so many life rafts I could toss down to those willing to be saved.

The retreaters arrived from their office jobs, stepping out of Priuses and Teslas and Leafs, eyes wide open, heads swiveling around and around excitedly, confusedly, looking, searching, scared, solemn, petrified.

Most of them stood against walls looking jealously at those cheery, more comfortable minglers. When you'd approach them, the nervous ones, they'd unfurl all the terrors and torments of their lives on you like you were their knight in shining armor, birthed only to provide them a solace from the too-cold world they wished to be a part of, yet were too scared to enter. But then they'd realize that you were actually talking to the person beside them and they'd withdraw, vowing never again to assume that someone cared about their worries and troubles, at least until the next time they were approached.

The sound of a gong rang out and everyone filed into the auditorium.

A wooden barrier ran down the middle of the room. The men were asked to sit in the rows of chairs on the left, the women on the right. A stage stood at the front of the room, and Mr. Joey Joy waited behind the lectern.

He looked out into the room of rabbit-like people, ready to spring out of their chairs in whatever direction they were told, with his welcoming and infectious smile. He began his speech.

Ladies and gentlemen: First and foremost, you are all loved. I want you all to know that I see each and every one of you. It might often feel like you are invisible, and the world is blind to you, but that's not true, because I see you. I see you because I am you.

I was in exactly the same place many of you find yourselves now. I was also raised in those bleak, lifeless suburbs. I roved around and worked many jobs after college, trying to find myself and some kind of meaning. I farmed and did construction and worked in retail and in restaurants and in tourism. And I had a very hard time finding myself; I got lost.

But I'm here to tell you that if you follow your path long enough and trust people enough to let them lead you when your eyes have lost sight of your path, you'll find your way to your destination. I know that the world has made plenty of unkept promises to you, and you're correct to be dubious. But please, just for this weekend, open up your eyes and ears, your hearts and souls, to the possibility that it's not too late to fulfill those dreams. Because it really isn't.

Soon, we will hear from our great leader in this retreat. But first, a story.

It was long ago when all were happy, during the times when the giants roamed the Earth. Their enormous feet plodded down, creating deep crevices in the Earth with every step, terrorizing bunnies and people and giraffes below. Man was small then; he knew his place. He chased gazelles across prairies and forded rivers and meandered from shore to shore and back again, eating when it was time to eat, sleeping when it was time to sleep, finding cover when a storm came, hiding when the jaguars neared. The men hunted, the women foraged, the children ran about and listened on the knees of their elders to ancient tales of sorcery and bravery.

But one day the giants vanished, never to be seen again. The people were confused. A brave lad climbed the tallest tree, but he saw no monstrous torsos stretched out above the forest canopy. The seasons passed. Wise elders told tales of the menacing giants' enormous feet that etched deep chasms into the Earth, terrorizing everyone below. But the children leapt out of their grandparents' arms, running off to childhood delights full of slug races and tag and playing at serious grown-up endeavors like war and negotiation and raising a family. The giants were forgotten. The people looked around them. They were now the apex species in all the land. This was new. Sure, there were still the tigers and lions and bears, but they could be dealt with, especially with that great new ally, Fire.

The people's seasonal meanderings occurred less often. Woods were cleared, trenches dug. Walls went up. Granaries were built. Feast and famine were tempered. Math was created as the seasonal accountings of harvests were written into meticulously kept ledgers. Starvation ceased. And the people even resisted over-population and the resulting food depletion by implementing a strict three child policy. All was good. Really, all was perfect.

Too perfect. With the abundance of food came a concurrent rise in the attractiveness of everyone in the community. The men grew fabulous muscles, the women's bodies bloomed curvaceously. The children were fit and ripe. Even the goats and sheep rounded out and looked quite ravishing. Orgies were had, unspeakable, filthy, torrid displays of human and animal love and seduction. But no amount of sex could quench that tireless human propensity for distraction and lust, and the people chased tail and ass and anything else they could get their hands on, but none of it was enough; none of it was ever enough. There was a societal collapse into a state of bored, satiated but unsatisfied, nervous emptiness. The mathematicians still etched great numbers into their books, but the surety of the bountiful harvests had lost all of the old joys of security.

The people were lost. They had everything and valued nothing. They were without guidance. They needed someone to toss down a lifejacket or a rope from the safe haven of a seaworthy vessel.

Ladies and gentlemen, our times are not so different from those ancient times. We also have all our basic needs provided for. The question is this: What will be our meaning when it is not derived from the everyday struggle for survival? For several generations we have struggled to answer this question. Well, I have finally found our prophet, the one who will help save our entire species. Here he is, my future successor at the Happy Hotline, please allow me to introduce my dear friend, Jay.

The people stood and clapped as I took the stage. They looked perfect out there in the crowd. They were one body. With so much potential. It was my job to harvest it.

Hello, friends. You are all loved. We're going to engage in a lengthier discussion on our last day here. For now, we're going to go over some procedural items and then I'll leave you with one thing to ponder as we head into the weekend.

So, some things to note: Meals will be at eight, noon and six. After we finish here, you can go to the front desk and get your cabin assignments and bring your suitcases over to your rooms.

Men and women will be separated for most of the

retreat. They will eat separately and bunk separately. A couple of the sessions will be mixed, but aside from these, you are not to mingle with the opposite sex. I repeat, no one here is to mingle with someone from the opposite sex. This retreat is for inward growth, not for mating or external pleasures. You have to build your own sanctuaries for yourselves instead of going out and trying to have other people build them for you. It wouldn't last that way. One person would be carrying the load for two, and the temple would topple over, crushing both of you beneath it.

So, avoid that easy temptation. Instead, dig into yourselves and plant some roots deep down and build up from there. One day, we'll all be tall oak trees full of acorns, but the nature lovers among you will know that you can't cast your seed into the rich soils of the forest before you're a mature tree. So, the question I pose to all of you, and what I want you to really think about, is this: Do you want to be the tree that can prepare itself to give, or are you going to continue to be the squirrel on the ground who only takes and takes and takes?

We're all here to work on ourselves. I wish you all the best in this endeavor. Thank you all for committing your time and energy to invest in yourselves. This desire is severely lacking in today's society. So, remember, you are all loved and appreciated. I want you all to enjoy yourselves and to grow. I'll see each and every one of you throughout the retreat. I cannot wait to hear how you are all progressing and learning.

Please, do not hesitate to approach me. Thank you all.

They funneled out of the hall, chatting nervously. Joseph approached to speak with me.

Wow, the savior himself once again. What a pleasure to see you. I'm very excited for the retreat.

He came nearer, looking up at me with puppy dog eyes. I couldn't get rid of the guy.

Joseph, nice to see you again. You seem to be doing well.

Oh, you too. You must be killing it at the Hotline to be able to put on a huge production like this.

I'm doing okay, yes.

Jay, I have to ask you something. You realize that it's Valentine's Day and all these people probably wish that they were at home in front of a cozy fireplace with a significant other, right? You can't possibly think that these people are going to keep their hands off of each other, can you?

I took Joseph by the arm and walked with him down the hall, away from the others.

Of course I realize that Joseph, that's the whole point. As soon as we let these people loose they'll be all over each other, fucking in the woods, in closets, in bathrooms, behind the walls of the building, in the cracks and crevices behind the dumpsters, they'll forge on despite the cold in their lust and they'll find exactly what they're looking for. It's what humans do best.

Joseph looked up at me, shocked.

But Joseph, think about what will happen tonight, when the ones who don't get laid see all the other men and women coming back into the cabins with flushed faces, right after experiencing the fuck of a lifetime? They're going to be devastated. And they'll understand that they are absolutely the least desirable, most lonely loser people of all time. You see, those are the ones who we can save. And they'll be even more desperate and ready for us to save them. The other ones have no interest in being saved, anyway.

Joseph slanted his head. Well, I guess that could be one way to find the people you're trying to help. I'm not going to lie, that sounds a little intense to me, but hey, you're the expert. Well, I hope the retreat works out well. I'll see you around.

Joseph walked off, turning back around to size me up, thinking he had it all figured out.

Too bad he'd be working on himself so intently. Otherwise, I'd get one of the women here to seduce him, which would finally free me from his prying eyes.

Oh, well. He wasn't a real threat, just a nuisance.

Everything was going according to plan, and I couldn't wait for the retreat to get under way.

CHAPTER EIGHT

I bounced from session to session. We'd brought in specialists from all over the world to lead them. Pablo from Guatemala led the jumping-jacks meditation session. A Middle Eastern happiness expert led the group laughter session. Or attendees could let it all out with Fernanda from Ibiza in the group crying session.

The past lives app session was led by the Blissful Bureaucrat himself. He took great joy in this particular project. He welcomed the group and began his session.

Good morning, friends. You're all loved. My friend Jay here helped create this wonderful app that helps us delve into our former selves and comprehend who we are over a vast range of time. By doing this, we can forgo the small sample size of this current insanely confusing life we're trapped in. The app allows us to escape from these blinders we call eyes and expand the range of our vision to an immense, never before seen scale. So, I hope you all did your homework and read up on what you did in your past lives. What did you all learn from those lives that we can use to better live these lives we're trapped in now? Yes, you in the back.

Mr. Joy called on a young woman who overflowed with unharnessed energy. She was dressed in frighteningly short shorts.

Hi, I'm Shana.

The group responded with a collective: Hi Shana.

The group blanketed her with a chorus of: You're always loved.

Shana continued: I'm from St. Paul. I work as the social media expert for a local bank. I really liked using the app because it confirmed everything that I thought I was in all of my past lives. In my first life, I was a white falcon and soared over the sandy Sahara, stopping at beautiful oases for a refreshing dip. Then, I was a broken wheel on an old wagon in Rome, which was pretty boring, I'm not going to lie, but you know me, I made the best of it and enjoyed the serenity of the waste yard. Finally, someone put me out of my misery by using me to crush a tax evader. I broke under the force of tens of men jumping on top of me to torture and kill the criminal. Then, this one's my favorite, I got to be a cloud for a month, soaring over the plains and the seas across the world before I finally broke into billions of tiny beautiful raindrops over the Rockies.

Mr. Joy was pleased.

Wow, Shana, it sounds like you lived some very interesting lives. What did you take from learning about all of these manifestations of your past selves?

It really helped me to get over the loss of my dear dog Wesley and remember that I've been alone before.

I've had a great time even when I was alone, so I can get through this period now and enjoy it for what it is, and then when a new dogfriend comes into my life, I'll enjoy him too. But I'm okay waiting for a while. There's no hurry. He'll come when it's the right time.

That's beautiful Shana, thanks for sharing. You are loved. Anyone else? Please, go ahead, friend.

I'm José. I'm from St. Cloud. I learned that none of it fucking matters, that's what I learned.

Mr. Joy was shocked to hear this; he believed entirely in the app and its powers of enlightenment.

Woah, José, I don't want to invalidate your feelings, but why don't you tell us about your past lives and then we can brainstorm and help you find some meaning for this current life you're living. There's always meaning, José, even when it's hard sometimes to parse it out.

Bullshit. My past lives were all as fucking miserable as this one. First, I was a soldier in the Roman army and got decimated along with the rest of my legion because the general thought that the army didn't perform well enough in a battle, even though we fucking destroyed our enemies and only lost two men. Then I was in the Persian army and died of fucking dysentery; that was some bullshit. The next time around I was an Apache warrior and my chief ran us into an ambush and everyone got killed but me, but I got captured and fucking tortured with my intestines tied around a tree. Some crows ate my insides until I finally fucking died a couple of days later. Then I died in some fucking training exercise in Scandinavia because my partner didn't know how to fucking hold back during axe practice. In France at least I didn't die in war, but I was so horrified by the smell of the disemboweled little boys and girls who the fucking British castrated and killed that I decided to off myself so I wouldn't have to smell the stench of it all anymore. All my lives were pretty much like that. I fought in World War I and World War II; don't fucking ask me which side I fought for, but I died obviously pretty gruesomely in both of those. I got gassed in the first one and grenaded in the second. Then I died in 'Nam then in Iraq in the Gulf War. And then I got rebirthed into this fucking bullshit fucking cycle into this goddamn country and guess who's a soldier and back into war again? Before the app I assumed it was my fate to be a soldier; my dad and grandpa and great grandpa were all navy men, so it's in my blood, but I hoped that at least one of my past selves might've had the calm life of a farmer somewhere, just chilling and harvesting some vegetables. But no, it's always war and war and more fucking war. Nothing changes. Nothing means shit.

Well, that sounds like some pretty gruesome lives you've lived, but I'm sure there were good times in them too. What did the app say were the best moments in those lives?

Who fucking gives a flying fuck about the best moments in lives when you're getting fucking crucified in war every fucking time? Fuck the best moments;

there are no best moments. The best moments are lies we tell ourselves that we're enjoying even though we know that eventually it'll all turn up shit anyway and we'll die in war like we always have. Sure, I haven't died yet in this fucking iteration, but I'm in the reserves and you know we're probably getting into a war with fucking China in the next two or three years. I'll get called back and thrown into some fuckhole in Asia to die like a dog like all of my past selves have. That is, if I don't decide to end it all again myself, which some of my coward past selves decided to do.

Look, José, my dear friend, first of all, know that you and all of your past selves are loved. And that everyone here thanks you for your service.

A woman called out from the back of the room: I don't.

Mr. Joy was astounded. What?

I give him my love, but I don't thank him for his service. I don't fuck with the war.

Josie, you're really not helping right now. We must all be positive and together here. It's about supporting each other. As I was saying, we appreciate your sacrifices. Can anyone think of some meaning for José as he went through these great struggles as a soldier, defending all of humanity for all time?

Josie couldn't hold back. Bullshit, he wasn't defending humanity, don't peddle that American patriotic propaganda, don't lie to him or to yourself. He was probably the one going into foreign villages and castrating the boys and raping and killing the women. It's people like him that make this world such a tough place for the rest of us. It's hard enough finding meaning going through all the other struggles in life, but then you get a piece of shit of a human who makes you, in your favorite past life, have to hide in a broom closet and listen to the wails of your sister as she's fucked up the ass and there's nothing you can do about it, so you're traumatized forever. Life would be so much better if not for war; we wouldn't need to have this retreat in the first place.

Mr. Joy was seething, but he calmed his temper before speaking. Josie, you are loved, but if you're not going to be here to support people, I'm going to need you to leave. José, I think we can glean something from your experiences by considering one of the fundamental natures of humanity. Whenever we're in peacetime, it's easy to forget that war ever existed, but war is one of our natural states and it's something that we have to embrace and not hide from.

José lashed out. We're not at peace, we're still at fucking war; my boys are still over there in the fucking desert getting killed for no reason. And even when they do make it home, they're still at war fighting their demons and losing, killing themselves every day.

Of course José, you're right. But I think your friends struggle so much when they return from war because they're ashamed of all their pain and don't know what to do with it. At war, everyone has that pain, so they can get through it together. But when they return, the pain is still there, but the people at home can't feel the pain. They can't feel it because as a society we're so distanced from the existence of war. It's fought thousands of miles away. But if you look at history, including your own, José, you'll see how prevalent war is and that it's nothing to be ashamed of. And it's something that all of us have gone through in one life or another. We're all in this together. And once you understand that you're a part of this wonderful human fabric, you'll see that each one of us completes the other and that indeed, we each are one another. We sacrifice for each other so that others can have more time and opportunity to find their own meanings and joys. So, José, you and your past selves perhaps didn't reap the rewards of your sacrifices, but your sacrifices allowed others to fulfill their destinies. And because you're a part of this stitched quilt of humanity and you're touching a part of all the other people who are right beside you in this quilt we call community, you too have reaped the rewards of meaning that your neighbors have been able to attain thanks to your sacrifices. We're all individuals, sure, but we're also a community, which means that our victories are shared between all of us. So, you could've been off battling in war, but your fighting has liberated the rest of us.

What are you fucking talking about? What the fuck do you know about war? There's no fucking meaning in it. It's brutal and it's bullshit and there's nothing good in it. Go see your friends stabbed and tortured and exploded over two fucking millennia and come back and tell me that their deaths meant something because their kids back home got to play with their toys safely. At what cost? You go and peruse the battered, destroyed, burnt-down marketplaces attacked for no fucking reason and tell me that there was a purpose in that. No one's safe, no one's succeeding, nothing matters, the wars go on and on and on and we all keep fighting them because that's all we know how to do.

José, my dear, beloved friend, you're certainly entitled to your opinion, but I think that it will help you a lot if you can dig deep and try to find some meaning in your tormented past, because, I promise you, it's there to be uncovered.

Mr. Joy took a deep breath. All righty friends, we're going to take a little break and then we'll come back and share some more. But first, I want to share a great secret with all of you. After the retreat is over, hopefully in the next couple of weeks, our top app developer Seth is going to be rolling out an app focused on our future lives. So, we'll have our pasts and our futures all mapped out, leaving us with only the present. We're going to talk later about the tools we can use to harness these apps and make the best out of our current lives with all of the wisdom of both the past and the future. Okay, folks, let's reconvene in five. You are all loved.

I had to leave to go check on the lunch situation and make sure there were enough gluten-free and vegan meals; complaints kept coming in about all these fucking specific dietary restrictions that people just decided on having and didn't fill out on the forms beforehand.

I looked at José as I headed out of the room. He sat hunched over, his head shaking back and forth as it rested on his hands.

Poor José. If he could hang on until the end of the retreat, I had exactly the right meaning to bestow upon his weary soul.

CHAPTER EIGHT

It was time for Giuseppe to speak to everyone in the auditorium. He had a good story to share with the crowd. I hoped it would help them.

He took the stage and began.

I was just like all of you. I lived a normal life, going through the day-to-day grind. I worked for a wire service, where I was paid to disseminate my opinions to the world. I'd get some comments on the site, you know, rile the people up a little bit. Some larger syndications picked up my work and put it out to a broader audience. I mattered.

But the more and more I put out, the less I became invested in the work. I covered most of the important topics and ran out of things to say. I started to become one of those boring reactionary critics who leeches off of the goings-on of the real movers and shakers to stay relevant. That riled people up even more, but it was all empty mutterings. They didn't know it, but I did. It got formulaic. Something would happen in the world, an action or even a misguided word from one of those Big People, and I'd twist it and turn it around until some kind of bullshit response formed, which I'd toss out into the world. I stopped even thinking when I wrote; I kicked back with a can of beer and a cigarette and an essay would issue forth on the screen. Then, I'd send it to my editor, who'd send it out to the people.

Things went on that way for a while. A lot longer than I'd like to admit. I was on autopilot for years.

Everything changed on a trip to New York City when I visited my buddy Steve. We walked around Central Park smoking a joint, wandering and exploring, passing the picnickers and the squirrels. We had a good time and headed back to his apartment on the Upper West Side, where we listened to music and munched on some snacks. I had a long come-down from the high; I didn't smoke too often. There was a gradual transition from high to sober, but then there was another shift to some other wild unknown state. Something I had never experienced before.

Steve put instructions in a hat, and we played an improv game. I became a seasoned pilot in the cockpit with Steve, my rookie copilot. Steve asked me why I was high while I was flying and I told him that I was only as high as was necessary for such a serious undertaking. He asked me why I was flying the plane backwards through the skies and I told him that he clearly didn't know what flying was all about. He asked me why I was reading *The Complete Idiot's Guide to Flying* and I told him not to question his superior and that I could fly the plane backwards, upside down and blindfolded if I wanted. He stopped questioning me when we crash landed on a decaying colony on Mars.

I left the passengers and Steve behind and embarked on my own. I spent the night walking in circles around a floating planetarium in the sky. My progression in the maze of the stars propelled me forward in life to some unseen endpoint, which, when reached, would hurtle me backwards to relive everything over again in reverse. At some point in my meanderings I must have reached the end, because I found myself lying in a cradle in God's garden as a baby. God read an ancient text and rocked back and forth in a chair in the doorway.

So, I began my life over. But I remembered who I was this time. I was God's long-lost son Adam, separated from my home and my partner. I grew up and was a young man lost in a foreign land, clothed in a black tank top and a pair of cargo shorts. Although my clothes were light, I was trapped in these garments and longed to return to my previous naked closeness with God. So, I stripped naked and ran out of the room trying to find Eden, but I tripped and fell onto the vinyl floor. Suddenly, the floorboards opened up and my head peeked through the ground into the depths of hell. Singed by the flames, I turned over and looked upward to glimpse pearly white gates through the ceiling, but then I blinked, and everything crumbled into dust.

Steve helped me up and we stood together in the windswept desert, but I lost Steve in a dust storm and I was alone. The heat of the inferno rose through the desert sands as rain washed over me from the heavens.

A flood lifted me skyward and I approached the rising sun. The waters receded from under me and I toppled down from the sky, landing behind a wheel driving on a desolate road around and around a purgatory of city streets, trapped forever seeking a parking spot in waves and waves of cars and cabs and do not park here signs. Someone called out to me with the voice of a long-lost love, so I exited the car and found her naked in an oasis, and we were naked together just as we had been so very long ago in the garden. She held my hand and led me to Jacob's ladder, and I grasped the bottom rung.

My hands stretched out to climb higher up the ladder, but then they were subdued and shackled. I was tied down to a chair. I bit the ropes and wriggled trying to break free. God whispered in my ear and a wave of serenity passed over me. I closed my eyes and slept the sleep of a thousand years.

I woke up sometime later in the psych ward, completely sober. I told the doctor that I was fine. I could tell that we were still in New York City from the honking and sirens blaring from down below. I identified my friend Steve. The doctor let me go and told me that I shouldn't smoke weed anymore.

Steve drove me home. He illuminated the dark spots in my memory. He had clothed me again and again only to have me strip down naked whenever he turned his back. He tried to get me to sleep and tucked me into his bed. Dozing in a chair by the door, Steve woke up to the sound of my footsteps as I walked around and around in circles.

Rain crashed against the windows and echoed in the apartment. I tore out all of the towels from the closet to fashion a raft, but then left the raft and returned to my maze, while Steve folded and placed the towels back in the closet. And then we commenced playing the whole game over and over again. Finally, he drove me to see his doctor friend, who advised him to call the paramedics. She held my hand and ran her other hand through my hair, soothing me while the paramedics strapped me down and brought me to the psych ward, where they gave me sedatives and I finally woke up, sober and exhausted.

My empty cabin upstate waited for my return. The first thing I did was brew up some coffee. The steaming liquid poured down my throat and helped bring me back to reality.

After resting for a couple days, I sat down at my laptop to type up an essay for the paper. But no words came.

Weeks went by. My opinions dried up like they were caught in a summer drought. The paper had no money to pay a writer who didn't write. Yet still I sat at the keyboard, hands at the ready. But nothing came.

Finally, after holding off as long as I could, I relented to my burning desire to return to Eden. I couldn't do it in society this time, though. I didn't want to end up locked in the psych ward. So, I sawed a hole in the bottom of an Adirondack chair and attached a chamber pot beneath it. I also fashioned a rig from a harmonica neck holder to hold a joint with an ashtray underneath it. I put a three-foot-long straw into a jug of water beside the chair. Finally, I wove sailing rope around my body and slipped my hands through a pair of handcuffs. A box on the desk behind my hands would automatically open via a timer one day hence with the key to the handcuffs inside.

The high was fine. It was normal. I came down from it gradually and waited for my divine trip, but it didn't come. So, I sat in the chair for another 17 hours completely sober, sleeping and shitting and peeing into the chamber pot and sleeping and drinking from the straw, until finally the lock opened and I was free.

Steve, after much prying, told me what strain of weed we smoked, and I bought three ounces of it. The results were better; I went on my divine trips maybe one out of five times instead of perhaps once every hundred. I was tempted to set the locking device to open sooner so I wouldn't have to languish through the unsuccessful attempts for so long, but the successes were so potent that it was worth the wait when it didn't work.

I've gone on amazing trips on those lucky occasions. I see the inferno and the gates of heaven and the ladder and the oasis and I'm in all of them or none of them or I'm in a hospital with Jesus or a bar with Moses or a bachelor party with Wilt Chamberlain or riding motorcycles with Hunter S. Thompson or sitting in a hot tub with John Steinbeck, with my pee flying into the chamber pot turning into a gold moat surrounding the Lincoln Log cabin of my shits turning into a towering Medieval castle and we're all there, me, me and me with God, and me and me with every version of myself in deep meditation with every other version of myself with God, holding hands with me and God, until the castle eventually fades and the smell dissipates and we're back in the garden oasis together and we're naked and together. How could I not keep returning?

That's how I spent August and September. But then autumn crashed down hard from the heavens, not even changing the colors of the leaves but sending them falling crumpled green and dejected to the ground instead. The cold seeped in through the walls and my money ran out. I had to spend more and more money buying weed since my tolerance had gone up so much. That, combined with not working, left me in a fair deal of debt. So, I locked the chair, chamber pot, weed and joint holder in the shed. I sat down at my desk, forced some words onto the page, and cranked out opinions that would provoke the people and drive traffic to the paper's site. My paycheck came in the mail and I kept the heat on through the winter.

But then the snow melted from the ground. The skies opened up and the rains brought with them the green leaves of spring. Life returned to its full majesty. Squirrels ran around and bears stretched their legs after a long period of hibernation. I looked over my essays from the winter. They'd kept the heat on and the people occupied, but I didn't recognize even one of them.

Steve came up one Friday to visit. We sat silently cradling beers around a bonfire in the backyard. I made him some eggs as the sun rose and he ended up leaving early that morning after intending to stay the full weekend.

I went back to my desk to write. The sun glanced through the window. I sat up from my chair, went outside and lit a cigarette. The empty blue heavens stared at me through the trees. The weak high of the cigarette teased me. The keys weighed heavy in my pocket. I unlocked the shed and strapped in to ride my chariot back to paradise.

So, that's how I spend my days. I quit writing and started to go around giving speeches like these to keep the bills paid.

If there's one message I want to leave you kind people, it's this: Find your psychosis. You all know your paradise. We've all been there at least once or twice, if we don't go there on a daily basis. Maybe it's feeling powerful, like you're the king. Maybe it's complete submissiveness. I know one guy who gets off on doing charity and feeling like he's the kindest human being of all time.

For me, it's communing with God. It's definitely a unique paradise, and the vessel I use to arrive at my destination is a strange one. I'm not saying you should all go home and do drugs and strap yourselves to chairs. But you should find the vessel that will take you to your own personal Eden and you should take it for a ride as often as you can. Thank you all.

As the crowd clapped, I stepped out from behind the curtains of the stage. Can I ask you a question, Giuseppe? First of all, you are loved. Thank you so, so much for sharing your story. The one question I couldn't keep from entering my mind as you regaled us with your tale was this: If you keep wanting to return to God and you go to these great lengths for even a hint at such a return, have you ever considered going on an eternal visit to your creator?

Giuseppe's brows furrowed as he considered the question. I'm not going to lie to you fine people. I think about that each time I strap myself in for my trip. For now, I'm content with going on that ride, because I know the destination, whereas I don't know if I'll really reach God in the afterlife. I guess it's a matter of faith. Perhaps one day I will go on that final voyage, when my faith is strong enough.

Thank you, Giuseppe. I think your message is a great one that we can all emulate and strive after. We can all join God or, for the nonbelievers, find our own secular paradise.

I turned back to the crowd, soaking up the expecting look in their eyes.

Heaven is a place on Earth. We all have the key. So, what are we all waiting for?

CHAPTER EIGHT

It was Saturday night. The night of the play.

The script was perfect. The actors had been practicing intensely. I hoped I'd prepared the audience well enough to receive its message.

They were separated on opposite sides of the auditorium. Women huddled together in their seats whispering like schoolgirls. Eager glances were cast furtively from side to side.

The lights went out. The curtain came up.

Sounds of winter waves crashing against rocks. Stage lights on. A cloudy haze puffs out over the scene. An eerie purple hue dominates the room. Large cliffs loom over the audience. Salty sea water sprays into the crowd.

A homey cottage by the cliffs. Old-fashioned clothes for old bodies. The wife carries a bowl of salad to her husband. They quietly pick through the leaves and chopped veggies and smoked salmon. He washes the dishes. The couple is pulled around the stage on thick, visible cables.

They read in bed. Books are put down with a sigh. Then, dry noiseless sex under the covers. Don't tangle the cables. Good. They lay side by side smoking cigarettes, staring holes into the ceiling.

The man retrieves a letter from the mailbox. His wife comes out to him from the porch. He shows her the letter. They hug each other consolingly. Their cables snag. They flail around. Eventually, they get themselves unstuck.

They stand over a freshly filled-in grave behind the house. They wave goodbye to their daughter. They trudge back inside in single file. They sit down on the couch, facing the television. The purple haze is palpable in the air. You can even taste it. It tastes like rotten fish.

They sit on the cliffs looking up at the stars over the sea. A star steals across the sky. Neither bothers to point it out to the other.

A slow breakfast. No jobs to rush off to anymore. The sun winds circles in its tracks around the sky. Sex. They turn the lights out. The sun finishes its cycle. The gears turn over and the sun begins its cycle anew.

They stand at the edge of the cliffs, not looking down. The wife looks into her husband's eyes. He nods. Three, two, one. She jumps. He stands still. She doesn't turn around on her descent wondering why he hasn't joined her.

He walks into town. He's the only one whose cables are visible. Two old men sit outside in the park playing backgammon. Mothers lead children in and out of stores. Storekeepers rush out to chase the leaving families, handing the children lollipops. Young fishermen lug tackle boxes out to the shore. The man turns around and retreats homeward.

Back at the cliffs. A blast rings out. The gun slips from his hands. The body plummets to the shore, joining the limp wife's body.

Crows descend on wires from the ceiling, but the couple swats them away vigorously. The couple is free from their wires. The man rises and he's young and he helps his youthful partner to her feet. He leads her up to the height of the cliffs. They have a new start, another chance.

The sun sets over the sea. He bends down on one knee. But she shakes her head no. He jumps again. This time, he stays dead.

She can live her life now, unburdened. She heads into town. She meets an old mechanic. He teaches her to rotate tires and change the oil. He gives her a job and introduces her to his son.

Years pass. The sun rotates around and around the ceiling. A wedding is held by the shore. The couple dances together. The cables propelling them along aren't visible. The haze is gone. The room is clear. The sky is blue.

The sun keeps spinning. The wife holds her baby on her hip as she sets the table. He comes home in his scrubs and she eats while he scoops mush into the baby's mouth. She smiles.

They hop and skip from scene to scene. They send the baby off to college. They play on the ground with their grandson. The card comes in the mail. The grave.

The sunset. The town. The hug. This time, the cables don't get stuck.

Loud moaning; bodies quivering in the steam of the shower. Get dressed to play mahjong with a neighboring couple. Doubles tennis with another couple. They return home smiling hand in hand.

They look out over the vast ocean. The imprints of faded bodies remain on the shore below. They look at each other. She remembers the past iteration of her life. He remembers his. They wonder what the next life will be like.

Holding hands and looking into each other's eyes, the sun sets. The stars come out. A star shoots across the sky. The couple points it out to each other. Somehow, they both know it represents their deceased daughter, and that she's smiling down at them. They hug tightly. The curtain comes down.

There was plenty of applause. They liked the ending. Hopefully they understood the actual point of it, and that the couple wouldn't have survived up on the cliffs for long.

When I first conceived of the play, I considered hiring the actors to keep acting out the play even after the curtain had fallen, repeating endless cycles of life and death, happiness and unhappiness, all happening over and over again without end, without meaning. But then I realized that this was superfluous. The actors, as well as everyone else in the auditorium, were all already stuck in this cycle, and nobody could stop playing their roles.

I climbed the stage to address the crowd. Give it up for the cast and crew one more time, they did a great job.

Now, we're going to split into the optional activities. There's an open bar and concert in the dance hall, open to anyone. Or, you can stay in this building for our feelings circles. The men's session will be right here in the auditorium and the women's is in the Pleasant room down the hall. Please, follow your hearts and make the decision that will give you the most joy possible.

CHAPTER EIGHT

Dark clouds rolled overhead like a train buzzing through a station. But then the train screeched to a halt, the doors opened, and out dumped all of the passengers in a torrid downfall onto the already snowy platform.

The people dispersed according to plan. The forlorn and serious and desolate prophets sat in circles talking about the meaning of life in the safety of the timber lodge. There were stacks of firewood beside the fireplace, saved up for just a time like this.

The others were in the thin-walled party barn across the yard from the main building, dancing to a blues band as the storm howled outside. No matter; alcohol warms the soul. Storms pass.

As the sounds of revelry wafted from the dance hall to the lodge, more and more people left the lodge to try their chances at catching some ass. But the downtrodden and hopeless, knowing their lonely fate from years of experience standing in corners watching other people party in the thrills of life, these people sat down and dug deeper into their search for meaning, and we were there to hand it to them.

I encouraged Joseph to head over to the party, but he wouldn't budge. I even tried being his wingman, setting him up with a beautiful brunette nutritionist, but he was sunk too deep within himself trying to work on his soul. The brunette frowned and then skipped over to join in the party.

The booze flowed heavy that night. Ancient enmities were forgotten in the subsequent intoxication. Love was in the air. Everyone danced madly.

José pulled Josie in close and lost himself in her swaying hips. The music pulsed. She whisked him away to the women's bathroom past a man who was raking a stranger over the coals of the sink. She dragged him into the handicapped stall, sat him down on the toilet and hopped into his ready lap. The joys of lust echoed in the bathroom.

Her moaning grew louder. You are loved. Oh, you are loved. YOU ARE LOVED! Yes, you, you brute, you fighter, you soldier, you massacrer of women and children, you slaughterer of hounds, you victim of violence and disease, you tortured tormented tormenting soul, you, you, **you** are loved!

He grabbed her by the waist and pinned her against the wall with one arm. He splotched his seed in the dirty weeds of her groin. They stood there, chests heaving, facing each other. Her eyes were the steady seas of martyrdom. He saw why she hated war so much, peeking past her eyes into the depths of her soul. She had been his companion in all those tortured trying lives.

He saw her bent over his torn-up body, easing drops of water into his cracked lips. Then, she was bandaging him up after another fight. Next, he was wiping the blood off of her gashed thigh after their town was burned and pillaged. Then, he saw the pain in her eyes as she placed the body of their infant son in a shallow grave, and then he saw her resoluteness as he climbed his steed to head off to battle once more.

She held him for a brief eternity as he cried in her arms. But he remembered how all of their past lives went and, destined to his fate, left her in the stall to clean up her soiled garden. Later in the storm, she spotted him having a threesome. She wanted to join in but was caught up in her own orgy. She watched him enjoy himself and smiled.

Return to the dance floor to scenes of love and scenes of longing and scenes of lust. Two of a kind by two of a kind by four of a kind. They dipped their toes into the naughty waters of seduction, then dove headlong into deep pools of delirium. They swam deeper and deeper until they got caught in the dense sludge of debauchery.

One adventurous couple braved the storm to cavort on a blanket in the snow. The slight woman felt her large partner enter her and it felt good. She felt him inside of her. She looked up at the snow swirling down from the heavens and felt him inside of her. She heard him cough and wheeze and she felt him inside of her. He stopped breathing, but she felt him inside of her. She saw his eyes cross and glaze, but she felt him inside of her. And he toppled down onto her crushing her under his dead weight, but she still felt him inside of her. She tried pushing him off, but he was too heavy. The warmth his body gave her lasted only so long. The snow piled up and up and their bodies lay intertwined in the snow and she died with him still inside of her. They were the first the storm overcame.

Someone strode over to the window. A howler of a storm raged outside. The snow swept this way and that and the whole world was covered by it. They returned to the revelry.

The booze flowed and the merrymaking was grand. A couple loved each other standing up in the broom closet. Another pair loved hard against the vending machines. Nina and Vicki touched each other with hands of love on the dance floor. Fred and Tim sucked each other's loves on the couch in the corner. George filled Leslie's sweet love with his own big love. Allen and Abby and Martin and Marilyn and Skylar and Sydney and Taylor and Thad loved each other in every contortion and combination and position imaginable.

Mr. Joy had wandered over a little earlier to check out the music and he stood happily bopping his head in the corner, glad to see so many people so thoroughly enjoying themselves and showing each other how much they were all loved. This wasn't like one of those depraved orgies from the stories, where people had sex solely out of lust. This one was purely about togetherness and joy and love.

The power went out, but the party went strong. It

was still warm inside. The sun must've risen but it was invisible.

A cold draft seeped into the room, but the people hardly seemed to notice it. They were all huddled up in each other's warmth. Eventually, though, they started to get hungry. The booze ran out. Hangovers started knocking on their skulls. By then, the snow was piled higher than the doors and had become like a solid block of ice. Some brave souls tried to break open a path to the lodge but were unsuccessful.

The snow kept falling. The pipes froze and water stopped running. Mr. Joy tried in vain to maintain the people's optimism.

They started drinking their own urine. Let's not mention what they eventually resorted to for food. We'll just say that, when we finally got to all the bodies a week later, many of them were not whole. José was the only survivor. He recounted the story to us, his face holding the same doomed expression as always. He never told us what he did to survive, but it couldn't have been pretty.

Meanwhile, the people in the timber lodge talked in circles about the meaning of life. Fires burned in the fireplaces, spreading warmth. There was plenty of food to go around. There were plenty of bottles of water. The storm didn't bother us at all.

CHAPTER EIGHT

Before we could escape our refuge, we'd have to wait out the rest of the storm.

Four days the snow gushed forth from the heavens. At first, the pitched skylight overhead let us peek up at the waves of snowflakes floating down. But the skylight was by now covered with mounds of snow and we were entombed pleasantly inside.

The people with me were resilient and kept on talking and talking, endeavoring with their words and my speeches to find answers, but the same words appeared again and again, and they eventually lost their meaning and fell distorted on weary ears. Mantras were repeated over and over. They wound on and on, turning themselves over and over. Delirium crept in as the storm dragged on.

Why'd the chicken cross the road?

To get to the other side.

Why'd the person cross the road?

To get the chicken.

What came first, the chicken or the egg?

Bok?

Bok bokee?

I need to tell you something.

What?

You are loved.

Who, me?

Yes, you!

No, you are loved.

Really, though, you are loved.

You are loved.

You**'re** loved?

Yeah, you'RE loved.

Oh, youREloved.

Youloved?

Olived?

I lived?

You are lived.

You lived?

You lived.

You are lived.

YOU LIVED!

The circle of survivors burst into laughter. Shrieks of *you lived* rang out with a jubilant resignation. You lived? You lived. You lived! **You lived.** YOU LIVED.

The time for love had passed. The time for understanding had come. `

I peeked outside from an upstairs window. The snow had ceased falling. It had piled so high even Shaq would've been well submerged underneath it. It would be days before anyone made it out here, especially with all the phones dead.

Unlike the partiers in the other building, the serious retreaters withheld their chastity in their pursuit of meaning.

Finally, after a seeming eternity of waiting, it was time to bring the troops together and do some building, now that all the bricks and hands were assembled in one place.

Sitting down beside my acolytes, I launched into my speech. I made sure to wait until Joseph was out of the room, since I didn't want him to interrupt me with his positive bullshit.

We've done a great job here. I'm proud of each one of you. You've all dug deep into the depths of your souls and sought your meaning. But this meaning in and of itself is not enough. We didn't come here just to find self-actualization. Because you can complete yourself, but you'll still be lonely and unfulfilled. No one wants to be a hermit in the woods. We have to go out and find partners. Not necessarily romantic soulmates, but rather the platonic partners of our eternal suffering. We all have them. Reach back into your past lives and consider the people who've helped you in your soul's quest. The paths you've all been taking have led you to this very moment.

So far this week, we've been building a tower of meaning and finding our shared language. But we didn't do all this constructing to sequester ourselves while a flood washes away the rest of our brothers, condemning them to continue in their cycles of suffering. We built this tower to bring others into it.

We can stack victories and lives story by story and make the tower so tall that it will be a beacon unto everyone, and all can join in and be saved by it. That's the mission I set for you: Go out and save someone. Just one person. For, if we save one person, it's as if we have saved the world. Each person is a world unto himself. A world with his or her own vast orbit. And we can save him or her from that endless spinning around in never-ending orbit, around an uncaring sun.

And don't forget to save yourself as well. We don't have to suffer anymore, and we can't forget to care for ourselves like we care for others. Your lives have only been suffering until this point. But now, the time has come. We have all lived.

Three more days passed, making it a whole week for us to survive on the provisions of the lodge and our souls. The people were excited and spent the last days plotting and planning and building up the tower to make it ready for all of its eventual occupants. A tower of bodies it was to be, stacked up one on top of the other until it reached the heavens, a monument to God, an indictment to him for the travesty of creation.

From out of the scheming group Joseph approached with furrowed brows, a concerned note in his voice.

You know, Jay, I'm not so sure about the effect you're having on the people here. I was excited to come out here to the retreat to check out all the great things you've been working on and follow you on this great path you're on. And I've gained a tremendous amount from being here and getting to hear everyone's different perspectives on life, and hearing about everyone's different past lives has been so fascinating. But it's starting to seem like you're teetering on the precipice between enlightened fulfillment and absolute destruction. It's a fine line, and it kind of seems like you're slipping off the edge, if you haven't slipped down it really far already, and it's a hard ledge to climb back up. And you're responsible for a lot of other climbers who are all attached to the ropes of your words. I hope you're not dragging them down with you, if you are indeed on the far side of the cliff.

Joseph was getting to be too much for me. Say, Joseph, how's your writing going? You sold any of your novels yet?

He took the bait. No, not yet, but that's not really my goal, honestly. I've mostly been cooping myself up, crashing by friends, trying to work on my writing and myself. I don't have any delusions of grand success or anything. But I like writing. It helps me to try and figure out some questions that keep plaguing my mind and soul, you know?

No, I really don't know Joseph. Here's what I'll tell you, though: Don't open your eyes on me. You see my success and you're getting jealous and it frightens you, because I don't really give a shit about succeeding in the slightest, and you're so eager to become a big and famous writer, a modern Hemingway, and prove to yourself that your life has meaning, even though that girl told you she didn't want you and you know you're worthless. You keep building fantasy worlds in your head about who I am and what I represent and your imagination's gotten the better of you. Nothing's happening here. No one's teetering on any edge. I show people the reality of the meanings they already hold deep within themselves. That's all I do. Now, why don't you go and work on that Great American Novel you're writing?

Joseph slunk off.

I took a deep breath and looked outside. A couple of bald eagles soared in the sky, carrying twigs into a tall pine, rebuilding their nest.

A few hours later, after a week of refuge in our sanctuary, the plow trucks finally made their way out to us and cleared all of the retreat's roads.

José stumbled out of the dance hall, begging for food and water. The hall stank of sex and excrement and death. We found the bodies of the partiers and of Mr. Joy. I was in line for quite the promotion.

A brief flurry fell. The flurry ended and the clouds acceded the sky to a double rainbow, which signaled the peace that was to come.

Before the retreaters scattered out to their missions, people suffered through miserable, unfulfilled lives. They would keep on suffering until someone showed them the way out. After we spread our words of salvation, nothing would ever be the same.

CHAPTER EIGHT

A retreater named Alexander saved Father Benjamin. Before his advice was distorted for evil, Father Benjamin was quite happy in his ministry. Before Ken came in for confession, Father Benjamin's congregation came to him bearing the heavy weight of sin. Before Ken confessed to the brutal beatings of his wife, the Father lifted the heavy yoke from off his flock's back. Before Father Benjamin gave up on Ken, he had pulled many a man back from sin. This time, though, Father Benjamin directed Ken to hand himself in to the police. Ken didn't react well to the advice. Ken returned home and beat his wife until her heart stopped beating. And then he beat her some more until her battered body was unrecognizable. Father Benjamin still had hope of justice prevailing until Ken had his day in court. Father Benjamin believed that the world was generally a fair place until the judge declared a mistrial and Ken left a free man. Father Benjamin walked around his church muttering phrases from Job until Alexander handed him a noose. After looking down at his pulpit one final time, Father Benjamin strung himself up in the rafters. After Alexander placed

Father Benjamin's limp body on the dais, he strung his own self up. He lived. And he lived.

A retreater named Eli saved Jaime. Before Jaime's hopes bled out into the snow, she enjoyed the serenity of the woods. Before the wolf showed up, she found a cute little motherless doe. Before the doe's intestines were strung out on the white ground, Jamie fed it oats and corn from her hands. Before the wolf left the doe's torn apart body without eating it because its meat wasn't bountiful enough to provide satiation, Jaime let the doe sleep in her warm shed. Jaime fumbled the doe's intestines trying to put them back into its little body until Eli drove by on his ATV. Jaime never believed that nature could be so ruthless until Eli recounted seeing a bear do the same thing to a baby chipmunk and a fox do the same thing to an infant bunny. Jamie believed that humans were above this ruthlessness and could help animals and each other until Eli reminded her about war and animal slaughter. Jaime stared at her red-stained hands until Eli placed a pistol in her grip. Jamie's brain sat securely in her skull until the bullet dislodged it, throwing it beside the mangled remains of the doe. After Eli picked up the gun from Jaimie's lifeless hand, the red and pink mush inside his skull painted itself on the canvas of the snow. She lived. He lived.

A retreater named Rebecca saved Michael. Before the IRS came calling, Michael's music store did pretty well. Before they froze his assets for no discernable reason, Michael enjoyed teaching kids to play guitar and violin and piano. Before his lawyer told him that everything would be okay, Michael lived frugally and made ends meet every month. Before the court case took longer than it should've, Michael hoped everything would get sorted out before his rent was due. Before his store was taken from him, Michael had paid rent on time every month for 59 straight months. Michael believed that people were inherently good until the lawyer sued him for failure to pay his dues. Michael believed that everything happened for a reason until the bank foreclosed on his home. Michael slept in a cardboard box under a bridge until Rebecca handed him a container of barbiturates. After Michael swallowed half the pills, Rebecca laid him down in his cardboard box. After his breath slowed and then stopped, Rebecca lay beside the box and swallowed the rest of the pills. He lived. She lived.

A retreater named Frederick saved Tina. Before everything went to shit, Tina lived a happy life. Before she left the stove on one night, she worked in the marketing department of her favorite makeup company. Before the stove's fire extinguished but the gas continued to seep out, her sons Sam and Cam slept peacefully in their bunkbed. Before her husband tried to light a joint, Billy and Tina enjoyed a wonderful marriage. Tina thought her life was perfect until she returned from a late-night run to the pharmacy to a house ablaze. Tina staggered down the road head hung low, wishing a car would knock her into the oblivion her family existed in. She was not so lucky. She kept walking down the middle of the road, cars dodging her, until Frederick handed her a knife. She filled her scorched bathtub with water and slit her wrists. After Frederick saw her release herself from the long roads of her affliction, he hopped into the bathtub, lying opposite Tina, and joined her in that blissful oblivion. She lived. He lived.

A retreater named Kara saved Melissa. Before she was fired, Melissa loved her job. Before the market for her services evaporated, Melissa traveled to Boston and Cape Cod and Greenwich for work. Melissa hoped to prove her value to the company and maintain her position until she saw whole departments being let go. Melissa felt like her life still mattered until her boss told her there was nothing either of them could do. Melissa thought she might find another job until she realized that her company had monopolized the entire industry and there were no jobs to be had. Melissa sat down on her porch letting the frozen wind pierce her unfeeling skin until Kara guided her to an alternate path. After Melissa stuck a stainless-steel fork into an electrical socket while standing barefoot in a puddle of tap water in her kitchen, Kara removed the fork, turned the breaker back on, and stuck the fork back into the socket. She lived. And she lived.

A retreater named Nick saved Laura. Before Laura realized she hadn't caught up with any of her friends in months, she thought that the people in her life cared about her. Before she decided to run a test to see if anyone would reach out to her, Laura did her best to maintain her relationships. Before weeks went by without anyone contacting her, Laura thought that her friends enjoyed their relationships with her. Laura thought her friends might just be really busy until she saw a post on social media of them gathering without her. Laura hoped to reconnect with them until she realized that she was a burden to her friends and that they'd only pretended to like her for years. After Laura got a restraining order for stalking who she'd thought was her best friend, Nick consoled her. After Laura tied a plastic bag around her head, Nick removed the plastic bag and tied it around his own head. She lived. He lived.

A retreater named Omar saved Joe. Before he found out the truth about his parents' divorce, Joe thought his wife was his rock. Before his dad admitted that his mom abandoned him for no reason, Joe thought his parents split because of financial troubles. Before he realized he was becoming his dad, Joe remembered his dad was never in another relationship after his divorce. Before his wife left him for no reason, Joe realized that his dad only made it through all those painful years because he had Joe and his brother to care for. Joe thought that his unborn son would provide him with meaning until his ex-wife told him that she'd had an abortion. Joe was destined to live in his lonely misery forever until Omar led him to the roof of the IDS Center. Joe's body was whole until it split into a million shards when it hit the ground. After he saw Joe's body drop 57 stories, Omar followed in his protégé's fateful footsteps. He lived. And he lived.

A retreater named Jackson saved Lucy. Before she was saved, Lucy hadn't felt anything in a while. She didn't feel any emotions, or any desire to do something with her life. Nor did she have anyone with whom to share her life. After Jackson found Lucy, he realized how true were the words of the prophet. These people really did need saving from their depressing existences. Lucy was an easy person to save, and she so badly needed saving. After Jackson walked her home, he walked himself home. She lived. He lived.

A retreater saved a stranger. Before the stranger was saved, they felt that life was meaningless, and they thought it would keep feeling meaningless until a retreater guided them to the exit, after which both the stranger and the retreater got to escape from lives that neither of them ever asked for. They both lived.

Play the scenario over again and again, 59 more times. Find truckers automated out of jobs. Find men left at the altar. Find betrayed women. Find guilt-ridden cops. Find guilt-ridden robbers. Find the battered and beaten of the world. Find the common man. Find the sad, lonely ones. Find the ones who want to cry out for help but can't. And then find yourself.

And Chava stood up from studying at her desk in her apartment in the desert. She put on a blue dress. The Jewish-star earrings matched with it well. Since the funeral hadn't really happened, she hadn't really laid down her earrings on the grave. She still had them. She dug through her jewelry box past her grandma's pearls, her sister's hand-me-down watch and those Jewish-star earrings to grab a pair of red and black diamond-shaped earrings, which barely matched her dress. The gift earrings sat in their tomb, forever awaiting ears they'd never again have the chance to adorn.

It was a cool night. Before the moon came out, the stars glimmered overhead. Chava listened to a record until her boyfriend knocked on the door. After he took her into his arms and kissed her, she held his hand as they strode into the bright night. After they returned home from a wonderful date, they made love like people who'd forgotten they'd ever laid in the arms of another.

Oh, and the river? It was still frozen.

CHAPTER TWENTY-FOUR

"You think we have a case here?" Joseph asked Youssef.

"A case? Are you kidding? We have 162 deaths on our hands out of 179 people who survived the retreat. More suicides are reported every day. And the people have all been found with someone else who also committed suicide. Something malicious must be going on," Youssef said.

"We're going up against a juggernaut here. You're risking your professional, if not your actual, life going up against the Hotline. I need you to be fully aware of the risks before we start working on this," Joseph said.

"Are you kidding? This is the kind of exposé that can make a journalist's career. I'm 100 percent in this with you," Youssef said.

"Great. So, the 87 people who died in the storm were already ruled to be tragic but unpreventable deaths and besides, 273 other people died in the city during the storm. In a best-case scenario, we might be able to prove that the people who died in the storm did not die accidentally. But I think our best bet is to prove that there was a cult-like mentality promoted at the retreat, that Jay was the mastermind behind it, and that he directly caused the deaths of everyone who committed suicide after the retreat," Joseph said.

"Agreed," Youssef said. "You were at the retreat, so your testimony is key. But from what you've told me so far, there were vague insinuations about finding meaning in death, but no concrete directives."

"That's right," Joseph said.

"So, what we really need to do, like right now, is find someone who's still alive and who might have fallen into Jay's preaching, and interview him. If he says that he interpreted Jay's speeches as a clear directive to commit suicide, after also convincing someone else to do so, and that others from the retreat had interpreted Jay's words similarly, then we have a legitimate case. I think we can get Jay behind bars," Youssef said.

José wouldn't talk. The investigative duo hoped he might help in proving that the accidental deaths weren't accidental, but he just sat there shaking his head. He would kill himself with another veteran in the next couple of days. The duo would need to dig deeper to prove the suicides were Jay's fault.

Three people on the list killed themselves before they could be reached. That left only 13 surviving retreat-goers, including Joseph. He and Youssef tracked down Pepe just in time.

He was stalking a barefooted man slinking along

the shoveled sidewalks of the West Broadway neighborhood. Pepe followed the man around loops and loops of the town, trying to conjure the right words to entice the stranger to commit suicide with him. But every time Pepe started to approach the stranger, his social anxiety kicked in. He backed off of his pursuit, wiped the sweat from his brow, and began the process of building up his confidence anew.

Joseph and Youssef took their time approaching Pepe, as they didn't want to alarm him.

"Pepe, you know that you don't really want to do this," Joseph said. "You don't have to, bud. What's compelling you to try and do this awful thing that you have no desire to do?"

"But it's my mission. I have to do it," Pepe said.

"Who told you that you have to do it?" Joseph asked.

"I have to," Pepe said, looking into Joseph's eyes for validation.

"Pepe, you can trust me. Remember how we talked at the retreat about how your past lives were tough, but they were all trending upwards? And how this life might be tough too, but it sure beats drowning as a sailor enslaved to the Athenians? Pepe, you have to tell me, did Jay or anyone else from the Hotline reach out to you after the retreat?" Joseph asked.

"What? No. Didn't they call you too? I don't know. Leave me alone! I'm trying to enjoy a walk in this nice weather," Pepe said.

Joseph and Youssef returned to Youssef's car. It

was viciously cold. The sun was absent. The wind howled. The depressed stranger hadn't gone far in his tottering along the slippery sidewalks, so Pepe easily neared him and continued his cat and mouse game.

The sleuths trailed the odd couple in their meanderings for five hours. Finally, the stranger entered a shack beside the river and, turning around, motioned for Pepe to follow him in. Joseph dialed 9-1-1 on his phone, but Youssef said they should hold off on calling for a bit. They tiptoed to the side window and peered in.

Pepe and the stranger sat in opposite chairs. Pepe looked at the floor. Neither one spoke.

Hours passed. The sun set early as usual, though it had never really come out during the day. There was no moon. The cold seeped past every fabric of the many layers of clothes on Joseph and Youssef's bodies. They resorted to taking turns at the window, leaving the car running for one of them to warm up in while the other did his shift watching the two silent men.

Somehow, Pepe eventually saved the stranger. Or, maybe the stranger saved Pepe. Before the stranger walked over to his closet and pulled out the hunting rifle, he conveyed his pain to Pepe through telepathic despairing eyes. Before Pepe realized that the stranger felt guilty for his daughter's death, the stranger realized that Pepe felt guilty for his parent's divorce. Before Pepe blamed himself for his mom's death at the hands of his abusive stepfather, the stranger blamed himself for accidentally reversing his car while his baby daughter crawled in the driveway. Before the stranger blast his body to smithereens, Pepe and the stranger both understood that this was the only way to relieve themselves of their guilt. The deadening boom lingered in the air until Joseph heard his heart beating violently in his chest as he threw open the front door. Joseph thought his horror could not be surpassed until Pepe picked the rifle up from the stranger's and blew his own brains out. After the second blast finally dissipated from his ears, Joseph heard Youssef ask him why he hadn't filmed the double suicide for evidence.

CHAPTER EIGHT

I faced the press and told them what they wanted to hear. The rash of suicides that it appears are being undertaken by people who went on the retreat are tragic beyond belief. My heart goes out to each and every family affected. We can only hope that they're in a far better and kinder world than this cruel one that we still inhabit. But, as painful as it is to say, their deaths are no more tragic than the 48,000 other Americans who killed themselves in the last year. Our line of work is an inherently challenging one and we do our best, but the fact is that we operate under the hardest of circumstances.

There are a lot of people out there who feel like they're sinking in the middle of the ocean. So, we throw them a life raft loaded with plenty of great supplies. We try and entice them onto the raft so we can pull them in to our vessel. But the sad truth is that many people ignore the raft. They prefer to sink in the waters of martyrdom. There's nothing we can do for them. But I'll tell you this: No matter how many people shun the lifeline we throw out to them, we'll always throw the next lifeline. We won't let anyone drown out there who's ready to be saved.

That is the conclusion of my prepared statement. Any questions?

Yes. A barrage of questions. Answer them. Appease them. Comfort them. Give them the facts, again and again. Prove that it wasn't our fault. Talk about the suicide rate in Minnesota. Mention that suicide rates are actually down for the winter, despite regularly rising rates of 40.6 percent over the last 18 years. Remind them that the Hotline is the one doing so much to lower those rates. Ask them if they know that 0.5 percent of all Americans over 18 have made a suicide attempt. Point out that suicide rates are up amongst all genders, races and ages. Lecture them on suicide's prevalence as the 10th leading cause of death in the United States. Regale them with the story of Kiyoko Matsumoto, who, in the 1930s, started a wave of suicides by jumping into the fiery Mount Mihara volcano, leading to almost 1,000 copycats. These things happen.

Remind them that these people were depressed and at risk in the first place. I mean, who goes to a Valentine's Day retreat refusing any possibility of romance? Only the truly dejected and forlorn.

We did our best. The programs were great. The app was a resounding hit. No, we weren't at fault for the people who died in the storm, we've covered this many times already.

I looked back into the crowd of reporters. We must look at the big picture here. What is the Happy

Hotline for? It's here to bring happiness and meaning to the people our society has rejected and brutalized. We're the good ones. You're the ones attacking them, telling them that the world's an awful place. You all are the ones giving them anxiety and depression with your 24/7 news coverage, where you shout at them about all the wars and murders and poverty in the world and never report any positive or joyous news.

We've saved thousands of people from literally jumping to their deaths. We've had over 26 million individuals come to our programs all across the country and in our first two international headquarters in Stockholm and Tokyo. And now, thanks to our app, we're in hundreds of millions of people's lives all across the globe. And we'll have our next app out in a couple weeks. One day soon, the whole world's going to be coming to us looking for meaning, and we're going to provide it for them, as we have for the last decade and a half.

Give us some credit. Quit with the ridiculous allegations. Understand who we are and how difficult our task is and cut us some slack. Oh, and remember, you all might be the ones calling in one day needing saving. So, don't take the life-saving phones out of our hands. That is all. Be Happy, folks. You're all loved.

Jesus. They're a pain in the fucking ass, but at least the media's predictable. They'll buy it up and, with a little cash put into the right hands, it'll all blow over soon enough. Just wait for the next celebrity or politician caught sleeping with their maid, or the next natural disaster or unruly racist misogynist professor to speak out. The media will hop all over it and the people will forget we were ever implicated in any deaths.

Leaving the Wonderful Welcome Room, I nearly crashed into my assistant, Mary. Say, how are you Mary? How's the ad campaign going? Good, great. Say, you look a little upset, is everything okay? Your friend killed herself? Wow, I'm so sorry. I wish they would've called in to the Hotline. That's really a shame. You know what, why don't you go home and spend some time mourning. Come back in whenever you're feeling up to it. Don't worry, I can take care of the campaign myself.

I hustled down to my desk in the cave.

Let's see, I gotta make sure that Lynch is set up to do well in the Senate. Then he can finagle the lifting of the China tariffs. Which will keep the merchandise flowing across the Pacific. Then we can threaten to move the headquarters to Wisconsin. That'll get us our tax breaks from the governor. He'll fall in line just like the mayor did. It'll all be to keep the local economy going, of course. For the good of the people. The politicians are easy to buy up. I can count on them to take care of me if anyone tries to bring me in for a hearing.

Next, we'll have to set up the ads to explode in the big markets. Washington, D.C. and New York, of course. Chicago and Detroit. San Francisco and Los Angeles.

Finally, I must remind Joseph and his friend

Youssef who runs this town. Make sure the people hear the real truth. The truth they need, not the one the media wants to give them. That fucking Joseph. Time to deal with him once and for all.

CHAPTER TWENTY-SIX

Youssef sat down at his laptop. He gathered together all the stats from the retreat. By now all 179 retreaters who'd survived the storm had committed suicide but Joseph.

Youssef related Joseph's personal account of the retreat. He reported Pepe's insinuation that he was called and prodded to commit double suicide by the Hotline. He depicted the gruesome double suicide of Pepe and the stranger, Barry Kingston, brutally splattering their brains against the walls of Barry's shack. He even proved that although suicide numbers were up as a whole in both the state and the rest of the nation, there was a small but noticeable rise during February in Minnesota.

Perhaps a few of the retreaters might have offed themselves even if they hadn't gone to the retreat, but it was impossible that 178 would have, and that's not even including the 87 people who died in the storm. Correlation was not causation, but the statistics were too overwhelming to be coincidental. And it all led back to Jay.

Youssef picked up the exposé from the printer, bringing the warm sheets to his nose. It smelled like a Pulitzer. He held his head high as he passed his colleagues' cubicles on the way to the editor's desk.

Shouting barked out from the editor's closed office. A balding gentleman slammed the door to the office and shuffled past Youssef. As he neared Youssef, he donned a blue Timberwolves hat and looked down at the ground. Youssef heard him mutter something about keeping his morals and that this was the only time he'd ever done something like this. Just as the man passed into the hallway, Youssef turned for another look at him. Youssef shook his head and clasped his article tight to his chest. He hesitated in the doorway. Phillip the editor sighed and motioned for him to enter.

"Was that who I think it was?" Youssef asked.

"Is that what I think it is?" Phillip asked, motioning to Youssef's Pulitzer.

"If you mean the best article to come out of this paper since you started here, and the article that's going to put this paper on the map, then yes, it is," Youssef said.

"I'm sorry, son. I know you put a lot of work into it and that you feel very confident about it, but you're going to have to let this one go. It's above me. I'm sorry," Phillip said, holding up his hands.

"What are you talking about?" Youssef asked.

"Look, I know you're a good writer and that

you've really progressed in the last year, but trust me when I tell you to let this one go," Phillip said. "There'll be other great stories that you'll break in the future. Religious figures will keep sexually harassing their members and politicians will keep embezzling funds and hiding bodies. But this isn't the one that's going to win you that prize you're after. Not at this paper. And if you're smart, not anywhere."

"But if what you're saying is true, and that was the owner of the newspaper who was just in here, then *this* is the people in power burying bodies. And that's bodies stacked on top of bodies! Shit, we could build a fucking skyscraper with all the bodies I've got here! You know you have to print it. That's why we do this work, to give the people the truth! They need it! They deserve it! You know that covering something up is far worse than the injustice itself. The truth will get out!" Youssef shouted.

"It's not getting printed. That's the last time I'm going to tell you. Now, go back to your office and work on your next article. Forget who you saw and forget everything you wrote. I'll tell you what, I'll get you a press pass to the game tonight and you can do an article on Coach Thibodeau and how he's doing with the team's chemistry after trading away Jimmy Buckets. Have some fun. Don't take everything so seriously. That's all, thank you," Phillip said, turning back to his computer.

Youssef returned to his office and dropped the Pulitzer into the bin beside his desk. He stared out at the frozen Mississippi. It looked more still than usual. The bike paths were empty. The trees were naked. The ground was invisible, covered by layers of snow. It was getting dark.

He shook his head. No way. That's not who he was. He couldn't give up.

He sent the article to a colleague at the Times. No way they could print it, but the friend had a friend at the Post. They weren't touching it, but the friend of the friend of the friend was over at the Mirror and they didn't give a fuck about printing questionable shit. So, they printed it.

Youssef sweated behind his desk, looking at the article online. That was it. The truth was out for the world to see. It would slip into the right hands and the big papers would have to acknowledge it. There would be justice. There would be glory. He wasn't doing it for the glory, but you don't say no to it when it comes. He saw old Benjamin Franklin on that golden medal smiling at him. He knew he'd done the right thing.

He pored over the comments on his article. They were promising. Someone said they had a friend who killed himself after the retreat. Then another person said it happened to their brother. And someone else said it happened to their niece. Youssef saw them all coming together. There'd be a class action suit for the ages. He saw Jay trying to wipe his tears with handcuffs on his wrists.

Then someone called the unnamed author a fucking coward. How dare he maliciously insinuate that such a benevolent, charitable organization that had saved his and both of his friends' lives do something like this. A voice shouted out in support. Another screamed in ALL CAPS that he was a FUCKING CUNT WHO WANTED TO HANG JAY FOR SAVING ALL THE PEOPLE WHO WERE DRIVEN TO DEPRESSION BY PIECES OF SHIT IN THE MEDIA LIKE THE COWARD BITCH OF AN AUTHOR! A fire burned through the screen and leapt and snatched at Youssef's beard and he fell back out of his chair.

He lifted himself up off the ground. Peeking out of his office, he glimpsed Phillip on the phone shaking his head behind the blinds. He saw a vision of Phillip walking over slowly and asking him to please get the fuck out and he saw Phillip trudge back to his office to clean up the burning pile of shit that Youssef had left for him. He saw himself going into office after office looking for a job and being blackballed everywhere he went. He saw himself writing freelance articles about the local dog show and hating himself for it. He saw himself drinking more and more, something he'd promised his imam he'd never do again. He saw his beard growing longer and more untamed, along with his waist. He saw his wife packing her things and moving back in with her mom. He saw himself in endless court proceedings for slander. It was impossible to indict someone on slander, impossible, but he saw himself handcuffed and led off to jail. He saw himself getting stabbed in the back in the barbed-wire-fenced yard by someone he trusted, who whispered to him not to fuck over a place that just wanted to help people. And he saw Jay smiling at his press conference, assuring the public that everything was fine, that the Hotline had saved more people than ever this year and was opening new branches in Paris, Cape Town, Buenos Aires and Medellin.

Joseph came across the article. He hurried to the Tribune building. He got off the elevator. It was dark and empty. He found Youssef's humble office. He remembered how they drank glasses of sparkling grape juice there when Youssef was promoted.

An empty bottle of pills sat on Youssef's desk. Below the desk a paper cup lay on the floor. Beside the desk a bunch of papers looking like a Pulitzer were heaped in a pile in the garbage bin. Behind the desk sat a lifeless body.

CHAPTER TWENTY-SEVEN

It was also cold in Wisconsin, though the thermometers measured slightly higher temperatures than over in Minnesota. But damn, the wind was a killer. It came in off of Lake Winnebago and howled at you, biting you through however many layers you wore trying to protect yourself. Fon du Lac was hell this time of year, but there was at least the comfort of heading to the bar and seeing friends as soon as work ended.

Sophie left her psychiatry office and sat down in her car. She'd had a full day of helping people cope with the traumas of being a human in the modern world and was eager to head to the bar and drink some non-alcoholic beers with Jennifer and William.

She scrolled through her Facebook feed as she turned the key in her car. She saw a post that included an article about the Hotline retreat. She remembered her sister Bethany being excited to attend it.

Bethany had been caught in this deep pit and was scratching and clawing to get up out of it, but it seemed she was turned upside down and couldn't figure out how to find the light above. The DUI was rock-bottom for Bethany and things could only improve. Sophie knew that things would turn around for Bethany if she could just find the right people to help her help herself.

Sophie looked at the comments on the post about the retreat and was confused. The source seemed reputable, but everyone was all riled up. "This is baseless slander!" they shouted. "How dare you tarnish the name of such a wonderful institution?"

It was indeed a wonderful institution. The Hotline had helped Sophie out when she was struggling through a lack of confidence when she couldn't get pregnant. They helped her get her chakras in line and within a month Sophie had a little baby seed planted safely in her womb. She patted her bulging belly with a smile. Why would someone try and defame the Hotline?

She clicked on the article. Her mouth was agape by the time she finished reading it. It seemed everyone who went on the Hotline retreat was dead. It must be some mistake. The author must have a personal vendetta. Bethany would clear everything up.

Sophie called, but Bethany didn't answer. Come on, Bethany, pick up. No answer. Pick up, Bethany! This wasn't funny. What was going on here?

Sophie texted her husband Paul that she was worried and was leaving to check on her sister. She set off immediately to Bethany's apartment in Eau Claire. Paul was worried about his pregnant wife and immediately left to meet her at Bethany's.

Sophie drove like a madwoman. She swerved in and out of lanes. She stepped on the pedal until it scraped the floor. She was lucky there were fewer cops out on the roads than on the night Bethany got her DUI, and also lucky that the roads were plowed well.

Sophie pulled up to Bethany's small house at the bottom of the hill two hours after she set out on the normally three-hour-long drive.

Before she leaped out of her Subaru, Sophie felt a deep pit in her stomach. Before Sophie threw open the door, she could already smell the rubbery scent of decomposing flesh. Before Sophie bawled beside the naked body of her sister, she noticed the naked body of a stranger on the floor. Before Bethany killed herself, Sophie loved her more than anyone in the universe. Before Sophie found the suicide note signed by Bethany and Tiffany, Sophie grabbed the gun from the stranger's cold fingers. Sophie completely forgot about the article until she saw the name Jay on the suicide note. Sophie had never thought of committing a violent act in her whole life until she realized that this Jay was behind the death of her beloved sister. Sophie didn't know if there were any bullets left in the gun until she cocked it and saw a bullet fly out of the chamber and another one enter in its place. Sophie wouldn't stop hunting Jay down until he lay dead like her sister. After Sophie sped off, Paul pulled up to the house and witnessed the carnage. After Paul called the cops, telling them about the dead bodies and that he couldn't find his wife, Sophie never stood a chance.

CHAPTER EIGHT

It was the last game of the season. The stadium was nice and warm. The Target symbol was everywhere. It was plastered on the basket stanchion and flashed intermittently on every screen in the building. The Target Center was printed in red on both sides of half court.

Someday, I'd love to get the Hotline's clown logo plastered all over the stadium. See the clown up there against the walls of the upper deck, like it's deciding whether or not to jump. At the top of the stanchion would be good, too. Its disembodied head could hang there, looking dead and happy.

We could even name the stadium the House of Happy. It would be beautifully ironic, since the fans never leave happy. Actually, I guess the fans of opposing teams leave happy. And there are usually more of them than us, so maybe it would be an appropriate name.

The game started off well. Even though the star center Towns wasn't playing, the offense was humming and a Saric and-1 to end the first quarter left the game two points out of reach. Sure, the team was

36 – 44 and was going to miss the playoffs by over 10 games. And sure, the outlook probably wasn't going to be any brighter next year. But you never know. Maybe we'd stumble into a top lottery pick or somehow manage to convince a premier free agent that moving to the barren tundra up north to play for an incompetent franchise wasn't a horrible life decision.

It was important to end the season on a bright note. Leave the fans with a good taste in their mouth heading into a short summer, one that many of them might not survive.

But then the tires fell out, as they always did. After we took the briefest of leads, the Raptors' Chris Boucher hit a three and then finished a slick layup, and they were off and running. By the time the halftime buzzer finally, mercifully rang, we were losing by 22.

The Raptors laughed their whole way into the tunnel. Their superstar Kawhi wouldn't have to play the entire second half if he didn't want to and they could rest old man Gasol's knees for the playoffs. It must be nice having something to play for. Clearly, the love of the game wasn't enough for our guys, who slunk off wordlessly to the locker room.

The mascots finished running up and down the floor and jumping on the trampolines and dunking. It was time for me to give my little speech. The building was already three-quarters empty, and it wasn't because loads of people were buying concessions and taking a halftime shit. The fans didn't bother staying until the end with the game already decided, even if that meant going back into the cold night earlier than they had to.

It was a shame they'd all taken their kids and left; the players always gave away their sneakers, headbands, jerseys and everything else they wouldn't need in the offseason at the last home game. It was also a real bummer for me, since there were hardly any people there to hear the message I was ready to bestow upon them.

I strutted out to half-court. Hello there, fellow Wolves fans! There's not too many of you left after that spanking we took in the first half. ESPN has us at a 2.2 percent chance to come back and win this game, so you might as well all leave at this point. I will give you some uplifting news, though. No, the Hotline hasn't bought the team, at least not yet. But, even though the team's sucking now, and everything feels depressing in this never-ending winter, the Hotline has some good news for you fine folks. We're putting on an incredible May Day Festival in three weeks! We're going to have a Prince hologram! That's right, we're bringing the legend back! Your favorite living Minnesotan, Garrison Keillor, will be there to regale you all with some of his famous stories. And one of your favorite former Timberwolves, Kevin Love, is coming back to lead a Posting Up Mental Health Clinic. It will be a day of festivities and the celebration of life. We're also going to have a special, explosive surprise at the end as a grand finale. We can't wait for you all to be there. Now, let's cheer on our Wolves as they defy the odds and send us into the offseason with a nice comeback win!

They didn't defy the odds, but I stayed until the end of the game, like I always did. The Wolves sat back and let the Raptors' bench hand us another loss, one in a season of many. I didn't get too down, though. The festival was nearing and things were looking up.

There was still plenty to prepare. Gotta get everything ready for that ultimate send-off.

CHAPTER EIGHT

I emerged from the bowels of the stadium into the parking lot for executives, players and special guests. The meeting with the players was nice, but their lack of any sadness or shame after their embarrassing loss was demoralizing. They were even playing music in the locker room and some players had the gall to dance.

The general manager would have to scrap the whole team and start over. Coach Thibodeau, for all his intensity, clearly wasn't able to connect with the younger players, nor to motivate them. The Wolves would never get anywhere with the prevailing losing atmosphere. It was indeed time for a fresh start. For everyone.

My driver waited for me behind the wheel of my brand-new Mercedes. Stretching to grasp the handle to the rear door, I felt something jab into my lower back. I turned around and saw the crazed face of an overwhelmingly pregnant woman.

Sophie's eyes bulged and her finger trembled over the trigger. You killed my sister. Her name was Bethany. I want you to know her name. You might even meet her down there, where I'm about to send you. She was far from perfect; she had her struggles. But she was trying to work on them, and I think she could've gotten better and atoned for all her past mistakes if she had the right guidance. Only, she had the misfortune of turning to you for help. And instead of helping her, you killed her.

Lady, I've never killed anyone in my life.

You have, you've killed so many. I read the article. And I've seen the bodies. You're a disgrace to all of us who are trying to help people. You take people's trust and then crush them with it. Well, I won't let you do it anymore.

You know that that journalist was discredited, right? He's not even alive anymore. He was so ashamed of the lies he was peddling to the public that he killed himself.

I looked past her. You'd better pull that trigger now… Too late.

Shots rang out and a body lay prone on the ground, oozing blood. The cops neutralized her with a bullet through the head and one through the chest.

Justice was upheld. An innocent man was saved from the grasp of a deranged woman.

I stepped over her prone body, shook the hands of the two policemen, stepped back over Sophie, entered my Mercedes, saw a sobbing man run up to the body and cradle its head in his lap, and directed the driver to head off into the night.

CHAPTER EIGHT

The cave door was closed. Candlelight flickered against the painted walls. The echoes of a squawking parrot resounded over and over: You are loved, you are loved. I passed a dollar coin back and forth between indifferent fingers from left to right, right to left. I swiveled around and around in my rolling chair.

The man in the TV on the far end of the cave talked about the heavy snow battering the Midwest. A motor-boat ad came on the screen. Sales were up. People couldn't wait for the rivers and lakes to finally thaw so they could zoom around and dive from their kayaks and canoes into the copper Boundary Waters. The news returned showing the Timberwolves getting thrashed again. There was no talk about the retreat or about those courageous proselytizers and their disciples.

The deaths had heaped up as body piled on top of body. Yossi was buried. Aaron was in the ground. Mr. Kundin had his funeral. The partygoers at the retreat got what they deserved. The retreaters built their tower and were a beacon to the world.

Copycat tandem suicides were already happening.

Suicide numbers were up statewide. It was a long and cold winter in the whole region. Similar numbers were now seen in Wisconsin and the Dakotas. They'd continue to spread out and climb as the tower got taller and taller and more people could look at it and see its light at the top spinning around and around, beckoning them into its safe harbor.

It wasn't only them, though, who rested peacefully. The whole world was dead. Journalism? Dead. Justice? Dead. Hope? Dead. Community? Please.

For what, though? It wasn't for me. It was for them. And they were surely glad of not having to suffer any more. But the chorus of their appreciation, after ringing out so sharply, had lost its strength. Some people had figured things out when they were spoon-fed the truth, but so what? What was that worth? What came of it? It all made me want to put a bullet in my own head.

The gun store was nice and warm. The rifles stood proudly in their racks. They had fancy scopes that could center a target on someone's forehead from 300 feet away. Metal safes towered over the customers as they looked for their favorite gun.

Behind glass cases, a multitude of pistols sat proud, so small they could be concealed in the folds of a woman's dress. Fat shotguns waited for someone to buy them and put them to good use.

Five of the rifles beckoned to me. The clerk

loaded them onto a cart along with boxes of ammunition and stacks of magazines. The clerk asked if I was buying the guns for a group of friends. Maybe we were going on a hunting trip. Sure, mister. Something like that.

There really is no thrill like the thrill of hunting. When most people hunt, they try and bag their prey before it gets wind that it's a target. But I make sure that what I hunt knows I'm hunting it.

You see, there's this look you can find in the eyes of the prey when it first sees the barrel of the gun pointed at it. There's a sudden comprehension of what's about to occur. And then there's a brief instant of peace and understanding.

That's when the trigger has to get pulled. Before their eyes get big as their flight instinct is triggered. If there's any hesitation, they turn to scoot away to another pasture. They'll still get shot and die, but they'll die with the tortured agony of the temptation of escape. But that escape is a misleading temptation. Because there's nothing to escape to. There's another pasture, sure. But the hunter will track down the prey and the same song and dance will be played over ad nauseum. Only that instant of comprehension could bring them true peace.

The festival would be the final piece of the puzzle, unlocking the freedom from the clutches of this dance for so many. It had to be. It was the quickest and best way to reach them. It would be cold, but the thronged masses would warm themselves up dancing and drinking.

They'd come in the tens of thousands for the Prince hologram blasting away on his guitar and singing Purple Rain. They'd stay for the Hotline's patented Tai Chi Rave. I'd give them the speech they'd been waiting to hear all their lives, and then their eyes would be filled with peace and understanding.

CHAPTER THIRTY-ONE

Jay walked into his house armed with bulky green duffle bags in each hand. He returned to the car and grabbed another load out of his trunk. He shuffled back into the house. The door shut with a loud slam.

Joseph, who'd been hiding behind a bush watching Jay, biked down the icy streets to the police station. Several cops leaned against their cars eating sandwiches and drinking coffee. Joseph put the kickstand up on his bike, leaving it on the sidewalk.

"Excuse me, sir?" Joseph asked.

"Can I help you?" the tall cop asked.

"Who do I talk to if I think someone's planning an attack?" Joseph asked.

"What kind of an attack?" the young cop asked. "And how do you know about it?"

"Um, well, I don't know about it for sure, but I'm pretty sure it's going to happen. I know this guy who's been saying some dangerous things and leading people to kill themselves. I tried to get him to stop but he kept on doing it and people are dying and my friend also killed himself after the retreat because of this man's corruption. And now I followed him to a gun store and saw him leave with four bulky duffel bags and bring them back to his house. I know he's up to no good. He used to only hurt people with his words, but I think now he's going to go out and shoot and massacre people. You guys have to help me," Joseph pleaded.

"Who's the man you've been following?" the tall cop asked.

"I don't know if I should say his name. Don't you guys have like some kind of forms I can fill out anonymously or something?" Joseph asked.

"Kid, just spit it out," the young cop said.

"Well, he's a really important man who recently took over a huge company. And he's been using his power to hurt people, not help them. I know it for a fact," Joseph said.

"Jesus, you're talking about Jay from the Hotline," the older cop said. "Fuck, they keep coming up with these hairbrained conspiracies about him. Listen, kid, it makes a ton of sense for a man to go and legally purchase firearms, especially when he has lunatics like you stalking him and trying to get him in trouble with the law on baseless slander. Some woman tried to kill him not two weeks ago at the Target Center. You better quit coming up with these ridiculous stories. Get a job. Find something better to do with your time." The other cops chuckled, shook their heads, and returned to chowing down on their lunches.

Joseph biked back down the forlorn streets, head

hung low. A car honked and Joseph swerved and crumpled into the snowbank on the sidewalk. He pulled himself up and saw the dim lights of a corner store. He didn't bother locking his bike, instead leaning it against the light post. He stepped into the warmth of the store.

The aisles had candy and pretzels and chips and there were pots of fresh-brewed coffee and machines waiting to dispense hot chocolate. Joseph meandered up and down the aisles and finally approached the counter.

"Can I get a pack of Winston's, please? Thanks," Joseph said.

Back in the frigid outdoors, Joseph took the plastic off the pack, ripped open the paper lining, snatched a cigarette and brought it up to his lips. He reached into his pocket for a lighter. But there was no lighter. He turned to head back into the store when he realized a woman was watching him. She wore workout clothes, had a yoga mat tucked under her armpit and didn't seem to mind the cold.

"Excuse me miss, do you have a light by any chance? Oh, what am I saying, you look like you take good care of your body. You probably haven't smoked even once in your life," Joseph said.

"I think I do actually have a lighter somewhere in this bag," the woman said. "But what kind of a smoker are you not to have one?"

"Well, I actually quit a couple of years back. But I just really needed a smoke," Joseph admitted.

"Life's getting you down, huh?" the woman asked. "I'll tell you what, I'll offer you a trade: I'll give you my number if you give me that pack. How's that sound?"

"Look, miss—"

"Please, call me Eve."

"Eve, that's very kind of you to offer, but I'm fine. It's just one cigarette."

"Ah, but that's how it starts…"

"Joseph."

"That's how it starts, Joseph. But it's a trap. You start with one, and maybe you only smoke once a week. You enjoy it and tell yourself that you won't slip back into the old habit, but then your back starts hurting, so you start smoking once a day, and then something happens to you at work, so you start smoking after every meal, and then you get into some family shit and before you know it you're smoking a pack a day."

"It sounds like you're talking from experience," Joseph said.

"You're right," Eve said. "I used to smoke a lot, but I was able to wean myself off them. Now, I only smoke weed, on occasion. Look, Joe, it's not worth it, I promise you. Take me on a date instead."

"I prefer Joseph."

"Okay, Joseph. I promise you'll have a better time with me than if you stew by yourself smoking your cigarettes."

"But why do you want to go on a date with me? You don't know me. All you know about me is that I'm a guy who turns back to his vices when he's down on his luck."

"I don't know. I guess you just seem like a good guy, Joseph. Keep your chin up. I'm sure everything will turn out just fine."

"Geez, you're quite the optimist. From my experience things don't turn out so good. Or, if they do start to get better, that's right when the world smacks you back down and then kicks you again once you're down."

"It's all for the best, Joseph, even the tough times. Trust me. You have to take every challenge as a blessing. It's the only way. You can learn and grow from every obstacle in your way, even the ones that seem to loom miles high. Put your faith into the world and follow it down the path it leads you on and you'll end up where you need to be. Now, can I have those cigarettes?"

"Fine, fine."

"Good. You know, I like to ice skate. I hope you'll give me a call," Eve said, handing over her number and starting to walk away.

"Oh, and Joseph?" she asked, turning back. He looked back at her, holding his hand over his eyes to shade himself from the sun's glare. "Maybe you feel that you're up against a great force that you can't overcome, like there's some kind of monstrous tower looming over you, making it hard for you to keep getting back up when you've been feeling kicked down. If that is how you feel, try and remember that no tower has ever stood forever. I hope I'll see you soon."

CHAPTER EIGHT

The sun shone in the blue sky. The weather had started to warm from the negatives of January and February to the tens and twenties of March and now it was finally approaching the frost point. But the forecast for later in the week portended another dive back to the high teens. The fishing opener was on the precipice, but all the lakes and ponds and rivers were still frozen. The fishermen were getting antsy.

Crowds thronged at the gates, taking advantage of the brief glimpse of spring. They wore sweaters and shorts. Some donned sandals, though their naked legs shook whenever the wind blew. The beers and music would warm them up soon enough.

I'd set up the guns in the massive speakers. Wires were tied around the triggers, which extended to a pulling mechanism in the lectern. Two fully loaded rifles were stashed behind the lectern's lower closet, with eight additional magazines piled in a heap in the corner. Explosives were set up in trash cans dispersed throughout the crowd.

Beer began to flow and music blared out. The festival had begun. The sounds of people dancing and shouting and singing echoed to the rear of the grounds. Then, Prince's hologram arose on the platform and the celebration really got under way.

I crept up the stairs at the far edge of the stage to peek out past Prince's hollow form into the crowd of tens of thousands partying and partaking in the revelry. Soon, the purple clouds would dispense and float through the crowd, overtaking them. They'd delight in the spectacle. Then, the air would clear, and they'd finally have their eyes opened wide.

I descended once more to the dressing room and flipped through the script of the speech, the words ringing loud and clear in my head. I could hear Prince elevating the crowd into higher and higher states of jubilation. I tore up the pages and tossed them into the bin. It was time.

The whole history of humanity had led up to this moment. The people had been turned over and over on the wheels of time and forced to partake in the constant cycle of birth and rebirth and suffering and now it could all finally end, if only for a few thousand.

The dressing room door swung open and Prince's ghost passed through its opening with a non-ghost woman under each arm. Prince tossed me a wink as I headed to the stage. I thought I saw a quick movement behind a doorway through Prince's empty body, but the people were waiting for me, so I hurried ahead.

I wanted to feel excited, but I remembered the equally loud chorus of appreciation I'd heard after all the other times when I'd helped people. But their chanting had faded. Maybe my joy over this moment would fade too.

But that bridge could be crossed when we came to it. For now, a bridge over those familiar frozen waters awaited. The sounds of the people called to me like they were calling for their messiah. But then, the world became quiet.

CHAPTER THIRTY-THREE

Joseph stood over Jay, pointing his gun down at him.

"Get up slowly," Joseph said.

"Joseph? What are you doing?" Jay asked.

"I'm doing what I should've done a long time ago," Joseph said.

"You're right. If you'd done this a couple of months ago, you could've saved hundreds of your fellow retreat-goers. Not to mention all of their new friends," Jay said.

"Shut up and stand," Joseph said.

Jay looked past Joseph toward the stage. Then he looked into Joseph's brown eyes. Soon enough, Joseph would end this little charade and Jay could go and fulfill his mission. Jay's brown eyes seared themselves into the meek eyes of Joseph. Joseph couldn't bear the strain and his head lowered.

His gun lowered a couple of inches too. But then, just before it was too late, the sounds of delight emanating from Prince's dressing room brought

Joseph back to his senses. He raised the gun once more and motioned for Jay to start heading outside.

"Joseph, let's not play around. I know you think you're doing something valiant, but you're really just preventing the people out there from attaining their destiny," Jay said.

The air still reverberated with the crowd's festivities even though the stage had been empty for fifteen minutes.

"You have a fucked-up vision of the people's destiny. And who the fuck are you to decide it for them?" Joseph asked.

"I'm not deciding it for them, Joseph. I'm just helping them remember their destiny and giving them the means to attain it," Jay said.

"Alright, stand the fuck up already," Joseph said.

"Look at you getting all tough. It doesn't suit you," Jay mocked. "I remember your broken, pathetic face looking up at me on New Year's Eve. Don't pretend like I don't see right through this tough-guy façade to your frail core peeing yourself in fright."

Joseph gulped deeply. He pointed the gun resolutely at Jay.

Jay finally arose. Joseph tied Jay's hands behind his back and led him out past the gates into the parking lot, his gun pressed into Jay's lower back.

The crowd roared. Prince, after having quite the time with his new friends backstage, had retaken the stage for an encore. More clouds of purple floated out over the people and they danced and sang along with their hometown legend.

Joseph shoved Jay into the backseat of the rented sedan with the tinted rear windows. Jay rested his head against the seat, knowing that Joseph was incapable of executing whatever ridiculous plan he'd concocted.

CHAPTER THIRTY-FOUR

I had set up the shack by the river for its prisoner. The chair sat waiting in the middle of the room with a bedpan beneath it.

We'd be here a while. There were a lot of things to sort out. I shoved Jay down into the chair and wrapped the rope around him, tying him down.

The easiest thing would be to kill him. But I didn't know if I had it in me to do that. To take another life. That's why I used the airsoft pistol.

"What's that?"

I looked up, surprised. "What?"

"You used an airsoft pistol? Jesus, you fucking rookie. How did I believe you that you were actually a threat? You're a fucking scared peasant like the rest of them."

I shook my head, trying to come to my senses. "Was I talking to myself?"

"So, you were never going to actually do anything, huh?"

"I don't know. I've been turning it over in my

head. I could turn you in. Maybe they'd give you the death penalty, if you didn't pay them off again. But I don't believe in the death penalty. I think that people should be punished for their crimes, but that it's not the state's role to put anyone to death. It's too much power to give the state. And so many people have died unjustly because of the death penalty. But even if I did turn you in, corruption would just rule the day, again. You'd figure something out. I keep thinking about Eichmann and how he's the only person Israel's ever executed. He's the exception that proves the rule. But even he wasn't really a threat anymore; they were punishing him for his mountain of crimes. And you have the mountain of crimes, but you're also going to keep going on with it, so really it would be the right thing to do to kill you. And if the justice system's not going to do it, then I have to. But do I really want to have blood on my hands? Who am I to make that decision to end a life?"

"You're so soft. Just let me go. You're never going to do anything to me."

"Oh, we've still got plenty to figure out. You sit back and let me think. Let me know if you want me to pull your pants down so you can shit." At least I'd learned that crazy idea from the retreat.

"How kind of you."

"You know, there's something I've been wondering about you that I'd like to find out. Let's put your fingerprint into the app and see who you were in your past lives."

"You don't have to put me into the app. I'll tell you. I'm the snake. The original cause of sin. The ultimate seducer and tempter. The only truth teller there is. I'm neither Satan nor God; they're both beings that people came up with to convince themselves that their lives had meaning. I'm the only one actually here. I give the people the truth and save them from serving false gods who give them nothing in return. I give them salvation."

"Is that true? Are you really the snake? Was that your past life or are you still the same snake as from in the Bible?"

"Jesus, you really are a fucking idiot. You actually believed that app was legitimate? It's a fucking algorithm that spits out random shit that people eat up because they're so damn lost in this world that they'll turn to anything to tell them what to do and what their meaning is. I'm not a fucking snake. And the Bible's not real. Don't you get that it's all a sham?"

"Oh."

"Look, kid, let's try and speed this thing up. There's people out there waiting for me. Besides, the cops will be here soon enough. You can't kidnap the CEO of a major company and not have someone tracking you down. Why don't you tell me what your thought process is and I can explain to you why you're wrong and then you can let me go."

"Let me think for a minute."

"Who are you anyway, that you think you're so important? You're a writer, right? Did you ever finish your book?"

"Well, I've been working on it for a while and I'm almost done writing the first draft."

"What's it about?"

"Well, the backstory is that I got this book of challenges where one of the challenges was to pick your most deeply held belief and then take the opposite position and try to convince yourself that your most deeply held belief is actually wrong. My deepest conviction is that life's worth living, so my novel's an attempt to challenge that belief and prove that life isn't worth living."

"Very profound. So, what's it about?"

"It's about me confronting all these different selves that I have in me. I have to kill them off one by one until I can finally find my true self. And now I'm at the end of the journey and it's just the real me left, at least the version of myself that I think is the real me, but I'm still stuck with the last version of me that I have left to defeat. That last part is the fear I have that there's no meaning to life. I should just write this fear down on a page and then rip it out of my notebook and torch it. But I'm not sure what'll happen if I extinguish it. I'm scared it'll rip out the other good half of me when it goes. Without that pain and numbness for me to counteract, all the happiness and satisfaction I attain will always ring hollow, since I won't have that other aspect of myself to defeat. It's kind of like I need to defeat that last self with a thousand stabs rather than with one final fell swoop. Maybe that way, I'd be able to slowly defeat and subdue that dark part of me, and the better version of me would have enough time to get used to life without all the pain and darkness. I don't know. I guess maybe the book is done and it'll just kind of end. But I don't know if anyone would buy it. And I don't really know if I've convinced myself in either direction. And I don't know if my deepest conviction that life is worth living is really as true as I felt it was, now that I've challenged it."

"You know, you're exactly where I was a while ago. You're going to go down the same path as me. You're smart. You're eventually going to realize that life's not worth living. It's all a bunch of bullshit. But hey, there's a bright side. Once you finally kill yourself, your book will sell, and you'll get famous posthumously. No one's going to not buy a book about suicide and the nature of our fickle mortality after the author has killed himself. It'll be a best seller."

"Maybe, but I'd already be dead and gone and not around to enjoy it. So, who does that fucking help?"

"Oh, but it'll help so many. Kill yourself and your book will be read widely. You'll send everyone who reads it on their destined quest to find their meaning and join you in that painless destination."

"You don't get it. That's not what this is about. You think of yourself as some kind of Christ-like figure saving people and unlocking the doors of heaven for them to finally enter. Or maybe in your case, it's the doors of purgatory or hell you're opening, I don't know. Maybe you believe that life's not worth living because it's full of pain and suffering. Fine. That's kind of true, though not the whole truth. But how do you know what's beyond the grave? How do you know that the people you're sending to their death wouldn't have eventually ascended to heaven after they got through this life, if only they could've made it through the tough parts? You couldn't possibly know what happens, so how can you be so sure that you convince other people to lose their faith and possible salvation?"

"You're complicating it for yourself. Forget heaven and hell and all that. It's simple. I see people suffering and I help them. They want to do it deep down, but they're too scared. So, I give them the little nudge they need."

"If you believe in suicide so much, why don't you do it?"

"Give me a knife or some pills or a gun. I'll do it. It'd be better than being stuck here with you forever, listening to your endless deliberating, when we both know you're not going to do anything."

"No, I won't give you pills. You believe in suicide so deeply. You've gotten hundreds, if not thousands, of people to kill themselves by now. If you truly believe that death is the right answer to the suffering of life, then stop breathing. You don't need any knife or rope. Stop breathing. You don't believe life is worthwhile, so don't live."

"Fine. You think I won't do it?"

Jay closed his mouth and nose. He didn't take a final breath. His lungs quickly screamed out for air, but he suppressed his body's instinct to breathe. His face turned red. He closed his eyes and pulled his head down concentrating, forcing himself to not give in. His eyes opened again, smoldering, and I felt the hate emanating from his soul. Then, he opened his mouth and hung his head and his chest heaved in and out. The breath poured back into him. He looked defeated and kept his head hung. Finally, he lifted it and looked up at me, his eyes playing off indifference.

I just shook my head. "That's what I thought. Don't you get that your nihilism is completely useless? It's gotten you nothing. You've succeeded so greatly. You've gotten so many people to kill themselves without getting in trouble. You've risen up the ranks and are at the top of one of the biggest non-profits in the world. You could do anything you want. And yet, you keep going down this destructive path. Tell me, if I hadn't stopped you and you had killed all those people at the festival, what would you have done next? You wouldn't have been satisfied. All the dead people you're lying to yourself that you're saving don't give you the appreciation you desire. There's nothing in it for you. You're pursuing an endless pit that you'll never reach the bottom of."

"Will you make a fucking decision already? Either kill me or let me go."

"I could kill you. I could make you go dig your own grave, but you wouldn't do it because you're a nihilist and you're going to die anyway, so you wouldn't care enough to do it."

"True. And because you don't have a real gun. Joseph, be serious now. How are you different from me? Go ahead, kill me. You might as well do it; you'll be doing me a favor. You're the same as me. How don't you get that? You see this problem that we have, and you act and try and help people, just like me."

I laughed. "Right, you really help them. They're so much better for your help. Hm. I could slit your wrists and watch you bleed out, but then I'll probably get found out and waste my own life in jail. I could leave you here and let you starve. But I'd still maybe end up in jail for murder."

"You're going to end up in jail either way. Kidnapping's a pretty serious crime. And the Hotline's got great lawyers."

"I could cut your tongue out, then I wouldn't have to listen to you spout your bullshit anymore. Plus, you wouldn't be able to convince anyone else to kill themselves anymore. But you'd still be the leader of the Hotline and could write memos and manifestos. With that reach, you'd still do a ton of damage."

"We're starting to run out of options."

"I could cut your hands off, too. But then we're running into the same problem. You could get yourself one of those expensive eye readers and do the same shit."

"So, what are you going to do?"

What am I going to do? Any way it plays out, I can see life going on and on as before. I'll keep setting myself tasks and goals and keep executing them, or not, and keep going on spinning over and over in endless circles, and the rivers will freeze and the rivers will thaw, they'll freeze, they'll thaw, and there will still be those tasks to accomplish, and maybe the very act of accomplishing them is in and of itself a success, and maybe it's possible to build from one success to another, but the rivers will still freeze again, and it will go on and on and on — to what end?

I wonder: Are there character arcs in real life? Can we improve ourselves? And if we can, will we? Or are we just the same selves living through different, or even the same scenarios, doing different or the same things over and over again? Do our arcs only amount to a flat line in the end? Can we goad that line to climb upwards? And if we do, what's that really worth? Even if we live the most perfect, fulfilled, selfless lives, with heroic character arcs always rising and never diminishing even for a second, and we only improve and improve until we become angelic heavenly saints, will even such greatness amount to anything when all is said and done?

But there will still be that voice saying we're not good enough, or that our efforts are all in vain.

Is the best we can hope for to lock up our dark sides and throw out the key, hoping that the darkness never manages to break out?

CHAPTER THIRTY-FIVE

So here I am, locked in a shack by the river with myself. One self is standing, while the other sits in a chair. The clock above the stove ticks off the seconds, but it takes its time, as if there were a hundred seconds per minute. I could stay in the shack forever asking myself these questions, never running out of questions to ask.

The yard outside the shack is derelict. A rusty car sits on cinderblocks. But the grasses are green and starting to grow taller. A buck grazes in the yard, its winter antlers still standing proudly on its head. Grazing deep into the thicket of scrubs and mangled bushes, the buck gets itself stuck. It doesn't kick around, trying to free itself. Instead, it waits patiently for someone to come and rescue it, as if it knows it has a greater purpose. And it will be saved, in due time.

The river thaws so gradually, it's almost impossible to tell the exact moment when it starts running again.

First, it's subsumed by thick ice.

Then, the ice thins, but still appears full. It's thick enough that a snowmobiler might be tempted to drive on it, but he would surely fall through. An ice skater might also try to venture out onto the ice, but she too would crash through it. Perhaps a duckling could take its first steps on the ice without it cracking, and it would do well to practice walking, for it hasn't yet learned to swim.

And then, as the river continues to thaw, there's a time when thin sheets of ice float endlessly on the surface of the river like a million stars in a watery land sky.

Then, at some point later, a black bear shakes off the grogginess of its hibernation and peers down into the thing that used to be a river to discover that there indeed it is: a river; all the ice is gone.

And so, I, Joseph Joe Jay Joey José Yossi Youssef Pepe Josephine Josie Sophie Aaron Erin Kundin Kuttler, draw near to the end of my book. The time for asking questions, at least for now, has ended. I hope that I've found some worthwhile answers.

I step out of the shack and start for the shore of my make-believe, yet very real river. I hear the chirping of the birds and feel the caress of the wind and the warmth of the sun. I head toward the buck caught in the bush. It feels like a higher power has put the buck here for me to help it out. And it feels like I do have a meaning in this world, and I just have to go out and find it. And I think I will.

I untangle the buck's antlers from the bush, and it

leaps and splashes and swims across the river and heads into the trees.

It's nice to help a living thing. I feel like I'm a part of something bigger than myself, and that in helping another being to live, I've helped to sustain the very fabric of life. I know that I've been helped on my path, and that I've helped others along theirs. And I know that the strength I've helped instill in others will return to strengthen me.

I follow the buck down the hill and arrive at the river. I crouch down and scoop my hand into the water to check that it's actually flowing, and it is. The river is free of a lifetime of ice, and it's running as if it had never stopped.

The sound of it is divine. It sounds like life itself. So, I cup my hands around my ears like I'm a deer, amplifying the sweet sound of bubbling life as it runs over the freed rocks and branches soaking up the sun.

Destruction is still locked within me. I will have to deal with it, or it will grow again to overtake me. But, for now, I can leave it where it is, safely locked up. So, I strip naked and sprint into the river, plunging into its waters, which are so cold that they shock my body and brain until every fiber of my being feels colder than ice, and then I break through the surface, returning to the warmth of the sun flashing through the budding trees, feeling more alive than I've ever felt.

ABOUT THE AUTHOR

Joe Kuttler has built timber frame houses and worked on regenerative farms throughout the United States. His short fiction has appeared in *Mystery Weekly Magazine* and in the *Canyon Voices* literary journal. This is his debut novel.